Carter knew now he'd been set up.

Behind him, he heard a soft footstep and a muffled grunt. A millisecond later, a billy whipped into his kidney and the Killmaster buckled to his side, raising his arms to protect his head.

As Carter hit the ground and tried to roll, he saw the big man who had been driving the Cadillac.

Carter was on him in an instant, his forearms closed over his throat.

He only meant to black him out, but the fear of defeat made the man go for broke. He slipped a knife from his belt and brought it into position for a thrust at Carter's side.

"Drop it or die!" Carter hissed.

NICK CARTER IS IT!

"Nick Carter out-Bonds James Bond."
—Buffalo Evening News

"Nick Carter is America's #1 espionage agent."
—Variety

"Nick Carter is razor-sharp suspense."
—King Features

"Nick Carter has attracted an army of addicted readers . . . the books are fast, have plenty of action and just the right degree of sex . . . Nick Carter is the American James Bond, suave, sophisticated, a killer with both the ladies and the enemy."
—New York Times

FROM THE NICK CARTER KILLMASTER SERIES

NICK CARTER

KILLMASTER

Death Squad

CHARTER BOOKS, NEW YORK

*Dedicated to the men of the
Secret Services of the
United States of America*

DEATH SQUAD

A Charter Book/published by arrangement with
The Condé Nast Publications, Inc.

PRINTING HISTORY
Charter edition/March 1987

ISBN: 0-441-57292-8

Charter Books are published by The Berkley Publishing Group,
200 Madison Avenue, New York, New York 10016.
PRINTED IN THE UNITED STATES OF AMERICA

ONE

On the Vatican side of the Tiber, far from the bustle of Rome, near the Piazza Adriana, lay the chapel of Our Lady of Fatima. Behind the chapel was a tiny, nearly full, cemetery.

Pad in hand, the tall, dark-haired man moved from stone to stone. His gray eyes devoured names, dates, and family as he moved.

But the pen in his hand didn't touch the pad.

He sighed with exasperation as he rounded the corner and slowly walked along the last path.

He had been in Rome nearly a month. He had made the contact he needed; now all he required was a name, a date, a family.

And he needed it fast. In six days, Alfredo Diaz would be in Spain. And before Spain there was Alvarez in Washington, D.C.

Suddenly he stopped, his leather-soled, newly purchased Italian boots sliding slightly on the loose gravel of the path.

It was a whole family, and from the size of the stones, not a wealthy one. They came from a nearby village, and from the number of graves, the entire family was deceased.

He searched the stones, hoping, his mouth going dry.

And then he found it: a boy child, born 1950, died 1953.

Perfect.

He jotted everything down on the pad, and then wrote the dead boy's name in large block letters: LUIGI ANTONELLI.

Angela Scarpetti ran water for a bath. When the tub was deep and of the proper temperature, she scented the water and stepped in.

Lovingly she soaped her body until the damp sheen of her olive skin dulled with lather, much as it had when *he* had bathed with her the previous night after making love.

Angela Scarpetti closed her eyes and a smile of absolute serenity crossed her lips.

A man wouldn't know, but any other woman seeing Angela at that moment would recognize that she was in love. She had been in love for a whole month, almost from the very moment he had asked to share her table at a little café on the Via Veneto.

He was the most handsome and charming man she had ever seen. He had smoke gray eyes and Angela had melted the first time he turned them on her. The aura of mystery that hovered about him was deepened by the instant electricity that ran between them. His physical presence was like a magnet that aroused her body and bled her brain.

Angela left the café that afternoon in a daze. He had asked her to dinner that evening. And after dinner, they returned to her apartment and made love, love like Angela Scarpetti had never dreamed existed.

In bed he was a combination of animal and saint. It wasn't that Angela had never had a man in her thirty years. She had had many, more than she wanted to remember.

Angela Scarpetti was not a very pretty girl. She was also constantly overweight. She was also constantly lonely, searching for someone who would love her back.

And he had.

They made love every night, and each night was better, more exciting than the last. Sometimes—more often than not, she had to admit—he frightened her with his intensity and the power in his body.

But always, afterward, he would calm her fears.

And then he asked for the favor, and Angela's worst fears were realized. She knew that she was being used. He had only loved her because of her job.

Angela was the chief clerk in the Rome Ministry of Records.

The story he told was convincing, however, and she did love him. Try as she might, she couldn't stop that.

She needed him. She needed anyone.

He told her he was Sicilian. It could have been possible. His accent was strange, like no Italian she knew on the mainland.

He said he was a soldier in the army of a don on the island, a Mafioso. He had failed his don and his adopted family. To make matters worse, the police were also after him. He wanted out. In fact, he had to get out to live.

And to do that he needed a new identity.

It would be a small thing to do if Angela really loved him.

And, oh, how Angela really loved him. The woman had become consumed by him.

She heard his key in the lock and her hands began to tremble.

"My darling . . ."

"In the bath!"

And then his handsome face was before hers. Their lips met and Angela couldn't suppress a tiny groan of desire.

"You are so beautiful, *carissima*."

She knew it was a lie, but his presence could make it a truth. He saw beyond the skin. He had found her inner beauty.

She hoped.

"You have them?"

"On my dresser."

He moved back into the bedroom, and then she could hear him tearing at the envelope.

"They're all there, and recorded—birth certificate, identity card, passport, military discharge, everything."

"Perfect."

And then he was back, leaning over the tub. His hands cupped her breasts, sending fingers of electricity through her entire body.

"You'll leave me now, I suppose," she murmured.

He said nothing.

His hands moved up to gently caress her shoulders and then her throat.

"Luigi Antonelli lives," she whispered.

"Yes, my darling. And because he does, Angela Scarpetti must die."

His fingers curled in the dark mass of her hair. She was forced down, into the tub, until her head was beneath the water.

She struggled, but she was no match for his strength. Only when she was still, when there were no more bubbles working their way to the surface, did he release her.

Carefully he went through the apartment, removing even the slightest evidence that he had ever been there.

Three hours later he was on a flight to Montreal.

From there he would rent a car in his own name and drive south into the U.S. and the state called Maryland.

It was noon. Ambassador Cesar Alvarez finished packing his briefcase and walked into the outer office. His personal secretary, Milena Silvado, looked up from her typewriter and smiled.

"You're leaving early?" It was a silly question, but she always asked it. Alvarez left every Friday at noon and didn't return until Monday.

"Think you can run it for the rest of the day, Milena?"

"Haven't I always?" the tall redhead replied.

"You are a jewel, my dear. See you Monday."

"Sir . . ."

"Yes?"

"Is the rumor true . . . about President Baldez?"

The ambassador forced a smile. "He's ill, yes, but not to the extent the rebels and the opposition party would have us believe. Just scare tactics. Monday."

Alvarez took the elevator down to the embassy garage. His Mercedes was waiting, the motor purring.

"You won't be needing a driver, Your Excellency?"

Another rhetorical question. Every Friday for the past year, Alvarez had driven himself to the lake cottage for the weekend. It was the only time he could be alone and regain his sanity.

He shook his head, got into the car, and accelerated up the ramp to the street. He forced his mind to remain blank until he was on the beltway, and then the old fears and frustrations flooded back as he remembered his secretary's parting question.

Old Carlos Baldez had made the country prosper. He had been a dictator, yes, but a benevolent man. His land reforms had brought a new standard of living to the peasants. The country had practically paid off its foreign debt.

But now Baldez was ill. Alvarez had lied to his secretary. El Presidente was gravely ill. If he should die, the logical successor was young Ramón, his son. The boy was a little wild, but he was well educated and smart. As minister of trade in his father's cabinet, he had done an excellent job.

Yes, Ramón Baldez would make a good leader. And it would be up to him, Cesar Alvarez, and Alfredo Diaz to make sure the transfer of power from father to son was peaceful and complete.

By the time he turned onto the Baltimore Parkway, he had pushed the headaches of politics and diplomacy from his mind. They were replaced with the expectation of a good weekend of fishing.

The main body of the town seemed to be north of the old highway, and he could see that there were a few stores still open on the main street. There was one small motel with a Vacancy sign out, and up ahead a service station and a restaurant made an island of light in the darkness.

He sighed and shifted his tall body in the seat. It was warm enough, even close to nine o'clock, to have sweated his ass until it stuck to the upholstery.

At the gas pumps he stretched his legs and rubbed hard at the cramped muscles in the back of his neck.

A tall, stooping man slouched toward him from the station. "Fill 'er up?"

"*Si*, please fill. Could I get a sandwich?"

"Yeah, sure," the man replied harshly, his eyes telling the story that he didn't like foreigners, especially spics. "Better hurry, though. She closes up in ten minutes . . . and she always closes on time."

He sauntered on into the little restaurant and haltingly ordered from a tired-looking waitress.

"Por favor, retrete?"

"Huh?"

"Toilet?"

"Back there."

He took his time, even washing his hands twice before returning to the counter. The sandwiches were in a paper bag. He paid and went back outside.

The attendant was waiting, drumming his fingers on the car door. "Twenty even."

The man gave him a fifty-dollar bill.

"Shit, ain't ya got nothin' smaller?"

"Lo siento, no . . . I'm sorry."

"Shit." He slouched into the station, banged at an ancient cash register, and eventually returned with the change.

"Gracias."

"Yeah, you too."

Across the street he checked into the motel and paid in advance.

"Just one night?"

"Si, yes, one night."

"Ain't ya got no credit card?"

"No, no card."

"Well, if ya make any phone calls, don't try to sneak off in the mornin' without payin'. Checkout time is eleven, sharp."

"Sí, gracias."

It was obvious that the old woman didn't like spics either, even if this one was good-looking as hell.

He carried his bag and the package he had picked up from General Delivery in Philadelphia into the room. He unwrapped the package, and, while he ate his sandwiches, he assembled the rifle.

Cesar Alvarez had driven slowly and stopped in Belts-
ville to eat. It was nearly dark when he pulled through
the gates and approached the house. He sighed in contentment as the Mercedes purred along the winding
drive.

It was the only investment he had left in the United
States, and one that he would probably keep even when
he was recalled. Since Baldez and the rest of the government in his country had become stable, Alvarez had
transferred his and his late wife's holdings back home.

But this place was very special to him, a haven from
the hysteria of Washington politics, even if a trifle os-
tentatious. The palatial, two-story, multiwinged residence sat on a ten-acre lakeside tract. Behind it was a
wide lawn that sloped down to a pier and a boathouse.

Alvarez was a widower, and the elderly gardener/
handyman who maintained the grounds and did odd
jobs around the huge, rambling residence lived with his
married daughter and her family. He quit work at five
o'clock each day to drive back to the city.

They would be alone.

He parked the car behind hers and smiled up at the
light shining in one of the upstairs bedrooms.

He was a foolish old man and he knew it. But then he
had earned the right to be foolish, and it *had* been four
years since his wife's death.

And then she appeared at the window. She might just
as well have been nude, the way the light shone through
her sheer negligee.

She waved, and Alvarez hurried into the house. He
dropped his briefcase on a hall table and rushed up the
stairs. She was waiting for him, naked as the day she
was born under her nightgown.

"Hello, darling. You're late."

"I stopped to eat," he replied, shrugging out of his jacket and tugging at his tie. "Your husband?"

"I told him I had to take some documents to New York for you. He doesn't expect me until tomorrow afternoon."

"You know, Milena, we're not being very sensible. If the opposition party in my government knew I was having an affair with my married secretary . . ."

"Shhh. Come to bed!"

Discovery. He shuddered at the thought. Yet a sense of danger and wickedness added an element of pleasurable excitement that swiftly dispelled his fear. Milena had ignited a spark of youth and adventure inside him, making life seem new and bright.

Then she was up and tugging him toward the bed. They fell together, locked in a fierce, straining embrace. His hand found one of her breasts, felt it rise and fall beneath his fingers. He cupped the soft, swelling mound, then gently squeezed.

Milena moaned and stirred beneath him. "Mmm, I like that, darling," she whispered. "Do anything you want to me . . . do *everything* to me!"

He leaned over her and began to unfasten the nightgown. His fingers were trembling and awkward. She lifted herself up slightly to help him undo it and their hands touched, then worked together to undo the catches and snaps that bound her.

In what seemed an instant she was totally naked, a sculptured white marble figure seductively waiting on the bed. He stared hungrily at her nudity as he slipped out of his trousers.

She saw him looking at her and gave a throaty laugh.

"Like what you see?" she asked softly.

"My God," he muttered thickly, "you're lovely . . .

so beautiful you take my breath away."

She had a voluptuous, womanly body with ample hips, a smooth, rounded belly, and perfectly tapered thighs. He thought of his wife and wondered how her slim body would appear in contrast to Milena's, then cursed himself under his breath. This was no time to be thinking of his wife. It was to rid himself of his desire for her that he was giving in to this girl's insistent demands.

He stared again at Milena as she lay provocatively stretched out on the bed. Their eyes met and locked, hers wide and imploring, his bright and full of male lust.

"Cesar," she whispered, "please, darling, do hurry."

Her hips twisted impatiently and she reached up her arms. He sat on the edge of the bed and kissed her hard on the lips. While his tongue probed the warm softness of her mouth, his hands explored her.

"Oh, yes, yes, Cesar," she crooned when he pulled his mouth away, "you don't know how good that feels."

"This is madness," he groaned.

"Yes . . . now hurry and make it complete madness."

For a brief instant her eye flickered to her purse on the bedside table, and she felt guilt. The telex inside had been cryptic:

President Baldez has taken a severe turn for the worse. All indications only a matter of time. Imperative you return at once. Also imperative you locate Rámon Baldez. Unable to reach in London.

No, Milena thought, there would be time enough, later.

He smiled as he dropped the powerful binoculars from his eyes. It would make an interesting scandal when they were found. The woman was an added plus they had only recently found out about.

He jacked a shell into the chamber and brought the rifle to his shoulder.

The bullet left the muzzle at just over three thousand feet per second. It was a forty-grain slug, copper-jacketed hollow point, designed to disintegrate on impact.

It did . . . in the upper center of Cesar Alvarez's back.

It was a full five seconds before the woman sensed that the mess covering her was blood. When she did, she went into hysterics. She tumbled the body from her and came to her knees on the bed.

With her hands over her face she stared down at the gaping hole in the man's back and continued screaming.

Without rushing, he jacked a second shell into the chamber and aimed again.

It was a classic shot, much easier than the first because she was higher in the light and the shock kept her stationary.

The slug entered her left temple at a velocity of just over two thousand feet per second. On impact the bullet began to smear and disintegrate.

Because the bullet traveled much faster than the speed of sound, Milena Silvado never heard the sound of the rifle shot that killed her.

TWO

Her hair was like a billowing black flag behind her against the stark whiteness of the newly fallen snow. Skis, boots, and stretch suit matched the snow, so only her hair gave any indication of speed and movement.

But even with such a small clue, her audience of one could detect the style and grace that made her downhill progress a ballet on snow. That arching dot of shimmering ebony became one in fragile harmony with the hostile side of the mountain.

Then she disappeared, but only for a moment. Suddenly she was over a crest and outlined against the sky, her body etched white on blue and framed by the soaring peaks of the Sierra de Cazorla.

The landing was perfect, skis parallel, poles folded, body tucked in a racing crouch. Then one last jump from the backside of an icy mogul and she was lost in a cloud of white powder less than a few yards from where he stood in the opened door of the chalet.

Their eyes, hers a deep, vibrant green, his a watery, tired brown, locked for a bare moment before she bent and deftly unsnapped her boots from the skis.

"Beautiful exhibition. Was it for my benefit?"

"Of course. You know how I love to show off for you."

12

She jammed her poles into the snow and stepped out of the locks and into his arms. The scent of her hair and the familiar aroma of her perfume as she nuzzled her face into his neck intoxicated him.

With a finger he tilted her face up and dropped his lips to hers. The kiss was long and filled with passion. He broke it only when he felt a shiver go through her body.

"You're shaking . . . come inside."

"It's not from the cold," she said with a laugh, brushing past him into the narrow entryway. "Bar's there. Fix us a toddy. I'll change." She scurried up the stairs and he moved to a portable bar.

"Any trouble getting away?" he called up to her as he fixed their drinks.

"No, but I have to be back in Madrid early Monday morning."

"So soon? Can't the minister of finance take one extra day off?"

"I have to fly to Paris to fetch Ramón. We are both ordered home as soon as possible."

"Oh? Is he off chasing young girls again?"

"No, the same one he has been chasing for about a year. I finally had him tracked down to her uncle's villa in Fontainebleau."

"Must you forever wet-nurse the future *presidente*?"

This time, when she spoke, she was right behind him. He turned to answer, but the words clogged in his throat.

Her beauty had been doing that to him for over a year.

Her raven black hair was extremely long and brushed to a glinting glossiness. She was unusually tall and strikingly sleek, yet sensually voluptuous. He was sure from the light filtering through the silky peignoir that she was wearing nothing beneath it.

He saw her eyes lift and catch him staring at her. Something in the pit of his stomach stirred. Something deep in his body responded violently to the sight of her. He could not look away. Her eyebrows were quite arched and her nostrils flared sharply. She held her red lips slightly parted and they glistened as though constantly moist. There was a sparkle to her teeth and her eyes were a peculiar color of green, curiously fathomless and cold.

"I love you, Alfredo Diaz," she whispered huskily.

"And I you," he gasped, catching her as she practically jumped into his arms. "We have only tonight. Let's make the most of it."

"We will," she replied, brushing her lips across his and doing wild, wonderful things to his body with hers. "Is your wife going to Paris?"

"No, she's flying home from Madrid in the morning. She thinks I have already left for Paris."

"Then I'll meet you in Paris. It will give us at least another day together."

"It would be dangerous."

She smiled. "Everything we do is dangerous."

Her breath was warm on his cheek and faintly flavored with mint. He saw very close to him the flicker of her dark eyelashes, and he inhaled her perfume with delight.

She kissed him hard, making him feel breathless and giddy. He felt soft inside, and a continuous sigh kept welling up in his throat.

He was lost and he knew it. The proof was that he didn't even care. He was recklessly eager to give himself to this woman, to do anything she asked, no matter how the affair might end. Even if it ruined his political career.

"I'll be at the Château Boulange in Fontainebleau."

"Can I call you there when I arrive in Paris?"

"Yes. Say that you are my wife."

"And now?"

"And now we have tonight."

He caught her behind the knees and lifted her. "The bedroom?"

"It's an open loft . . . the top of the stairs," she breathlessly replied.

By the time they were on the bed, they were both shuddering with excitement. A throbbing pulse pounded inside the head of Alfredo Diaz, making him feel dizzy and weak. Although the room wasn't warm, sweat rolled down his forehead and into his eyes.

"Take it off me," she cried with exasperation, tugging at her gown, then turning so the ribbon sash was easily within his range.

Alfredo Diaz raised his hand and saw how badly it was trembling.

This woman was amazing. One minute with her and he forgot his dying *presidente*, the threat of the Marxist rebels in the hills of his country, even the threat of insurrection and betrayal inside his own cabinet in the form of General Emilio Cordovan.

But worst of all, she made him forget himself, his life, and his duty.

Then she was naked, moaning, whirling to thrust her luscious body against him.

"I want you!"

They tumbled to the bed, and as she rolled one leg over his body she glanced quickly up at the clock on the wall.

It was seven-thirty.

He would arrive at precisely ten.

She glanced back down at Alfredo Diaz, at his glazed eyes and thrusting body.

It would be simple to keep Diaz amused until ten o'clock.

She moved from the bed slowly, making as little movement as possible so as not to wake him. Without pausing in her movement she slipped the peignoir around her and padded to the door.

Once there, she stopped and looked back. He was sleeping the sleep of the sated, his mouth slack, his arm over his eyes to blot out the dull moonlight streaming through the window.

"Bastard," she whispered, and moved into the hall and down the stairs.

At the front door she flipped the cover over the peephole and fitted her eye against it.

He was there, a shadow in the trees that lined the narrow drive leading to the chalet. She flipped the hall light on and off, and the shadow moved instantly, running with catlike grace toward her.

What an animal he is, she thought.

She cracked the door just wide enough for him to slip through, and closed it behind him.

She had barely turned when his powerful arms enveloped her. The kiss was full of passion, lust, and desire, but it quickly ended and he released her.

There would be time enough for that later, their eyes said, when all of it was done.

"Maryland?" she whispered.

"It is done, not a hitch. They shouldn't find them until sometime tomorrow afternoon."

"And you checked into an inn here?"

"Yes. The concierge should have no trouble identifying me. Have you been careful here?"

She smiled. "This is the only thing I brought other than my ski clothes. The fool didn't even notice that I had no bag. This is all he cares to see me in anyway."

"I can see why," he quipped. "Fingerprints?"

"I have touched nothing without wiping it clean at once."

"You learn the game very fast, my darling."

"Our little game, my darling," she replied, sarcasm in her tone, "has been a long time in the planning. Ramón is in France, the Château Boulange in Fontainebleau."

"The same woman," he said and chuckled. "This time our Ramón must really be in love."

"It's a shame Nina Boulange will be a widow before she is a bride. Here is the number. I got it from his briefcase."

"Where is he?"

"Still in the bed, sleeping . . . top of the stairs."

He reached out and ran a finger over the tips of her breasts. "How often I have imagined you with him."

"You're perverse," she hissed, but maintained the smile on her full lips. "Now get it done!"

As he moved silently up the stairs he screwed a silencer into the barrel of a Russian-made Stechkin pistol.

Gently he shook the shoulder of the man on the bed. "Diaz . . . Alfredo Diaz."

"Huh . . . ?"

"Wake up, Diaz!"

"No, sleep some more."

"Wake up, you bastard, or you'll sleep forever."

The drowsy man's eyes cracked and then opened, instantly alert to the muzzle of the Stechkin inches from his forehead.

"You!"

"Yes, Diaz, your secret police just can't seem to kill me." With his free hand he fumbled a sheet of paper from his pocket. "Read this a time or two to get familiar with it."

Diaz scanned the sheet and shook his head. "I don't understand . . ."

"You don't have to," the man said, already dialing the phone. "Just don't ad lib too much while you're talking to Ramón Baldez, and hang up when I tell you to!"

Diaz took the phone in both hands and swallowed hard as he heard a woman's crisp voice on the other end of the line.

"Château Boulange."

"I would like to speak to Señor Ramón Baldez," Diaz said in halting French.

"Who is calling?"

"Alfredo Diaz. It is an emergency."

"One moment."

Diaz felt the gun press behind his right ear. "It was a maid or secretary. She's getting him."

"Stick to the script, Alfredo!"

"Hello, Alfredo, I got your message. I'll have a car meet you at Orly tomorrow—"

"No, Ramón, I must meet you Tuesday night."

"Tuesday night?"

"Yes, Ramón, it is very important. We must meet alone. You must come alone to the Café Tito on the Rue St. Blanc. Do you know it?"

"Yes, but—"

"It is an emergency, Ramón. Ten o'clock Tuesday night. Will you be there?"

"Yes, Alfredo, of course . . . but—"

"I can't talk anymore now, Ramón . . . Tuesday night, ten o'clock."

The phone was snatched from his hand and dropped to its cradle.

"You should have been an actor, Diaz."

"You rebel scum!" Diaz hissed. "I didn't think Chango would go to such lengths. What are you planning—"

The rest of the sentence never left his mouth.

Three pops, like the explosion of champagne corks, burst from the Stechkin's silencer.

At a range of less than a foot there was no question of missing. The three slugs, practically fired as one, lifted the whole top half of Diaz's head off.

Carefully he wiped the gun clean and dropped it on the floor. He was whistling as he descended the stairs.

"It is done."

"I heard," she replied.

She was already in her ski clothes, pinning up her thick hair to go under the mask.

"I'll call you from Paris when it's over."

She nodded, and together they went outside.

"It's a good night for cross-country," she said, clamping on her skis and retrieving the poles.

"The next month may well be the most dangerous part . . . take care."

"I will, and then Porto."

"I will be making the arrangements," he said.

They kissed, and with a last embrace he walked down the lane and turned at the road toward the village.

Seconds later she was gliding down the mountain in the opposite direction.

THREE

As a young man of twenty-five, Esteban Vargas had been round-faced, almost boyish. His nose had been prominent, his eyes round and large beneath dark brows. They had been curious, inquiring eyes, trying to find meaning from life and his own scheme of things in a chaotic, rebellious world.

Now, at forty-five, after twenty years of fighting and living off the land in mountainous jungles, the face had become like the body, lean and hard. It had become a hatchet face, too narrow and long, and never smiling.

His movements were confident, his speech deliberate. The jungle fatigues he wore were clean but worn to threads.

This day, as Vargas stepped from the jeep and approached the small hut to meet his lieutenants, his shoulders sagged with an unnatural tilt. The eyes, usually bright and hard and confident, were filled with worry.

The interior of the hut was windowless and mechanically ventilated by a malfunctioning machine. Illumination from a single bare bulb hanging from the ceiling by a fraying cord cast a ghostly pallor over the eight men sitting silently, waiting at the round, rough-hewn plank table.

Vargas paused before seating himself, casting his eyes from face to brooding face.

Each one of them, at one time, had commanded over a hundred men. They were still outnumbered by the federal army, but using guerrilla tactics and with the peasants on their side, they had been more than a match for the federal forces.

Now these eight men commanded less than ten men apiece, and even their morale was fading.

Even a blind man—and Esteban Vargas was far from blind—could see that their glorious revolution was failing.

He looked around his "command headquarters" and barely suppressed a chuckle.

At one end of the hut was a folding table with one bent leg. On it were a metal coffeepot, a few chipped cups, a few spoons, and a tin of sugar. The walls were a dull brown, marred by scratches and gouges with black soot around the ventilation grills.

Three years before, Vargas had bragged that he would be running the country from the presidential palace.

Now he was still in this grubby hut, and not a single farmer or peasant had climbed the mountain to donate cheese and meat for the bellies of his men.

Vargas lit the stub of a cigar and eased himself into a chair.

"What is the latest on Carlos Baldez?"

There was general shuffling of feet and hands. Heads swiveled, eyes darting to meet other eyes and then quickly looking away.

At last one man stood.

"It is not good, Esteban. El Presidente has slipped further away. Our informants say that he is now in a coma. He does not respond at all."

Vargas nodded wearily. "A prognosis?"

The man shrugged. "Only a matter of time. It could

be hours, a day, most likely not a week."

"I see," Vargas growled, hauling himself to his feet and circling the table in a slouching stride. "And I suppose the generals dutifully sit at his bedside hanging on every breath the old man takes."

There was subdued laughter around the table, but none of it humorous.

"And, most likely, General Emilio Cordovan goes directly from the sickbed to the chapel and prays for the old man's quick death."

Again Vargas nodded and slumped into his seat. "Most likely. And this other, new wrinkle?"

A second man, stone-faced, leaned forward eyeing his leader. "Alfredo Diaz and Cesar Alvarez have both been killed, assassinated."

"And we will probably be blamed for it," Vargas grunted. "Are the Americans investigating?"

"Yes, but so far we have not learned what they know."

"Nevertheless, we know who is really behind it." Vargas paused and relit his cigar. "Gentlemen, when Carlos Baldez took office he was a fascist, not unlike his idol Franco in Spain. At that time we thought that his election was the final blow that would allow us to obtain power."

"Yes, Esteban, but the old man fooled us."

Vargas chuckled. "Yes, he certainly did. He restrained the military, he instituted reforms, and he gave the peasants what they wanted. In short, he eroded our power base. He did away with the necessity for revolution, even if he made himself a dictator and a rich man at the same time."

"But now, Esteban . . ."

"Yes, now it is time to lay facts on the table. Gentlemen, six months ago, before Baldez fell ill, I met with him."

"You what?" practically all the eight spoke at once.

"We met, just the two of us, secretly. We agreed that we would lay down our arms and come out of the hills. In return, our lands would be returned and we would have an equal voice in the government."

"The old bastard agreed to that?"

"He did. I think, in many ways, he trusted us more than he did Cordovan and his own generals. As you know, we have long suspected that Baldez held the military in check. He wouldn't let them launch a massive attack against us because he could play us off against his generals. In many ways, we kept him in power."

"And now Cordovan waits for the old man to die."

"And Baldez's two most powerful allies," Vargas said, "the two men who could insure that the old man's reforms would be carried on, are dead."

"And with their deaths, Esteban, does that mean that peace with us goes out the window?"

"Perhaps not. We, and the country, still have one hope . . . Ramón Baldez. Do we still have men on him?"

"Yes, Esteban, twenty-four hours a day. He is in France now at a château in Fontainebleau."

"I think we all know who is behind the murder of Diaz and Alvarez. It stands to reason that Ramón will be his next victim. With Ramón out of the way, Emilio Cordovan can take over the country within hours."

"We could give our suspicions to the Americans."

Vargas laughed. "Do you think the Americans will believe us?"

"What do you propose, Esteban?"

"That we get to Ramón first—kidnap him for his

own safety. How soon can you give the order?''

"It can be done in the next three hours."

"Then do it," Vargas ordered, rising. "I shall inform our contact in the capital. With the power of liaison President Baldez has given her, she should be able to help us get his son safely into the country."

Vargas stalked from the hut and climbed into the jeep.

"The village," he barked.

As they careened down the narrow mountain trail, Esteban Vargas felt a knot begin to grow in the pit of his stomach.

The killings of Alfredo Diaz and Cesar Alvarez had an all-too-familiar pattern to them. They were the mark of a professional. There were many professional hired killers in the world, but some sixth sense in the back of Vargas's mind was telling him that this particular assassin and his methods were well known to him.

Could it be that Benito Venezzio was alive?

And, worse yet, if Venezzio were alive, could it be that Vargas's old friend and comrade was betraying him?

Dominique Navarro stepped from the shower and patted her tall, sleek body dry with the large, European-style towel. She couldn't help but notice with disgust that the towel was badly fraying at the edges, as was the rug beneath her feet.

Her gaze drifted out the windows to the ten thousand acres that had been her birthright. It was now down to less than a thousand, and ninety percent of that was unproductive.

She closed her eyes and tensed her body in anger for several seconds. When she opened them again she was staring at her own image in the mirror.

"But that will change," she told the beautiful, green-eyed face staring back at her. "Even that will change!"

She was just pulling on a pair of slacks when the phone on her bedside stand rang. Instinctively her hand shot forward. Then she thought, and the movement was arrested. She waited, counting the rings. It died after the fourth. That would be Vargas.

She waited a full minute, going through the numbers in her mind and coming to the one that would ring in the cantina in the tiny mountain village. It was picked up on the first ring.

"It's me. Christ, I've been trying to get you for five days!"

"I've been in the capital," she snapped. "How do you think I sent you the news on President Baldez?"

"Regardless," Esteban Vargas replied, "you should stay in closer touch—things are happening too fast. You heard about Diaz and Alvarez?"

"No," she lied. "What about them?"

He told her, and she made the requisite moans and groans.

"No matter, perhaps we can still salvage something before the old man dies. Our people have located Ramón in France."

"Oh? Where?"

"Never mind. We had a meeting this afternoon. I've ordered our people there to pick him up."

"Pick him up?" she gasped. "You mean, *kidnap* him?"

"What better way to insure his safety? I'll need your help to get him into the country. Can you do it?"

"Yes, yes, of course," she said, her eyes flying to the clock, her mind calculating the time in Paris.

"I'll contact you as soon as we have him and he is on his way."

"Very well. I will start the arrangements."

"And, for God's sake, Dominique, stay in touch!"

The phone went dead and again her eyes darted to the clock. It was too late to reach him. He would already be in place. They had no contingency plan for such an event as this.

Should she call the general? No, better to wait and see what happened.

Perhaps his bullet would reach Ramón before the men of Esteban Vargas.

The rifle was a Mannlichter single-action CD-13. It was the perfect sniper piece, especially when fitted with a Startron night scope.

Once again, the contact had come through with perfection. The key had been in the rest room at Orly as per his instructions. He had retrieved it within minutes after clearing customs. A few minutes later he had gotten the customized case from the airport baggage locker and been on his way.

It pays, he thought as he began to assemble the rifle, *to have money, connections, and power behind you!*

He chuckled to himself and attached the specially built aluminum "stick" butt.

"Not like the old days," he said aloud, "when we had to work all alone and usually go through the nuisance of stealing one's equipment."

He opened the shutter slightly and looked down at the narrow, dimly lit street.

The Rue St. Blanc was more like an alley than a street. It ran in more or less a straight line from the wide Avenue du Maine and ended directly below the window. The front of the building opened onto the Rue

Froidevaux, which ran the length of the Montparnasse Cemetery.

That would be his route of escape when it was done: out the building's front door, through the cemetery, and to his car in the parking lot of the Lycée Paul Bert two blocks away.

The hollow sound of footsteps reached his ears from around the curve two hundred yards away. He pushed the shutter open a tad more and lifted the Mannlichter to his shoulder.

It was a couple, young. The man was dressed in jeans and a black bolero-type shirt with a fringed leather jacket.

He adjusted the Startron and read the scrolled designer's name above the breast pocket.

She was a thin blonde with tight curly hair and good legs. She was also wearing jeans, and a halter top that accented the youthful, jiggling breasts above it.

He narrowed the scope down to the ripple of her left breast and adjusted the distance as the couple approached.

When they were a hundred yards away—still twenty yards from the small neon sign that read Café Tito—he squeezed the trigger.

"Bang, you're dead."

When the couple had passed out of sight into the bar, he slipped three steel-jacketed hollow points from his pocket and lined them up on the windowsill.

Then he checked his watch and sat back to wait.

"What's he doing now?" Jesus Miranda said from his crouching position in the back seat of the car.

"He's parked, just sitting," came the reply from the front.

"Now he's checking his watch," came a second voice

from the front passenger seat.

"Shit," Miranda growled, "we should have taken him on the open road."

"Don't be a fool," said the car's fourth passenger, cramped into the seat beside Miranda. "He's driving a Jaguar. This is a four-cylinder Fiat. If he even smelled us, we'd lose him for sure."

Again from the front seat, "And this is the first time he has been out of that damned château for days. It might be our only chance."

"Then let's take him now!" Miranda insisted. "Drag him out of the car!"

"No, still too risky," the driver replied. "I want him in the open where it will be clean. Wait . . ."

"What is it?"

"He keeps glancing there at that alley . . . the Rue St. Blanc. I've got an idea. Stay put!"

The driver exited the car and was back in two minutes.

"It's perfect, if that's where he's going. It's darker than hell. Only two streetlights, and a bar almost at the dead end."

"A dead end?"

"Yes, and the street is very narrow."

"Shit, there he goes!"

"Jesus?"

"Yes?"

"Stay down, both of you, until I give the word. Here we go!"

He heard the footsteps before he saw the man, and steadied the rifle. Only two shells remained on the sill.

He was ready.

He centered the cross hairs in the Startron on the man's chest and floated the scope up to the face as the

figure walked into the illumination of the first street-
lamp.

Ramón Baldez.

He adjusted the scope as the man moved, dropped it-
back to his chest. The hollow point would shatter on impact. If it was a good sternum shot, there wouldn't be a
need for one of the remaining shells on the sill.

He was about to squeeze off the shot, when all hell
broke loose in the street below.

Two drunken revelers poured from the door of the
Café Tito. At the same time, a small green Fiat charged
up behind Baldez with its lights off. Three men poured
out of the car, all diving for Baldez.

The shooter's instincts were fast. He didn't know
what this was all about, but he saw his quarry quickly
disappearing.

The muzzle of the Mannlichter darted to and fro, trying to find an opening to Baldez as he fought with the
three men.

He fired.

And missed. The slug exploded in the rear door of the
Fiat.

Quickly he reached for one of the other shells.

Baldez's mind screamed "trap" the instant the car
doors flew open. He let his reflexes take over and went
on the offensive at once.

The first man who reached for him got a balled fist in
the gut that sent him reeling back against the car. By
then the other two had reached him and were trying to
pin his arms and legs.

Baldez hooked one with an elbow and then turned on
the other.

"Señor Ramón, come with us! It is for your own
good!"

"*Por favor, señor!* Hurry into the car!"

Baldez heard their pleas but paid no attention. He went straight for the one in front of him, trying to head-butt him out of the way for a clear run down the alley.

His head had barely connected with the man's chest when the car door, a foot from his hip, exploded.

"Christ, it's a sniper!"

"Where?"

"Somewhere . . . up there!"

"Everyone in the car!"

Two of them gained the strength of ten. They used their combined weight and the tentacles of their arms and legs to force Baldez into the rear seat.

"We've got him! Go . . . go!"

"Jesus . . ." the driver cried, slamming the Fiat into reverse.

"Jesus, get in!" screamed one of the men in the rear, covering Baldez's body with his own.

Jesus Miranda was the man Baldez had butted with his head. He had staggered into the far wall. Now he was on his feet and lunging toward the car.

He never made it.

Suddenly he screamed. His arms went into the air and his body lifted.

The car's occupants had no doubts. The entire left half of Jesus Miranda's chest had been blown away.

"We can't help him now. Go!"

The back tires screamed as the car roared in reverse toward the mouth of the street.

On the sidewalk, Jesus Miranda stared with unseeing eyes up at the night sky over Paris.

Dominique Navarro had smoked nearly a pack of cigarettes in the last hour. She had also consumed nearly a whole pot of strong black coffee. Every sound in the old hacienda made her jump.

When the phone rang at last, she nearly screamed aloud.

It rang only once and went silent.

It was he.

It was nearly a full two minutes before it rang again. She snatched it from its cradle before the vibration became a ring.

"Yes . . . ?"

"It's me. There were complications . . ."

"I think I already know. He was grabbed."

"Yes, how—?"

"Esteban told me earlier this evening. He called. There was no way I could reach you in time in Paris."

"What now? There is no way I can get another try at him."

"I've been planning all evening," Dominique replied. "This may work out even better. You go on to Zurich, to the doctor. I'll handle it here."

"You're sure?"

"You have done everything you can do, my darling. I'll do the rest. Spend our money wisely."

"Until Portugal."

"Until Portugal. I love you."

The connection was broken. She waited until the sweep-second hand on the clock had made one complete revolution, and dialed the phone. It rang in the private bedroom of Army Chief of Staff Emilio Cordovan.

"Yes?"

"Paris failed."

"My God!" he roared.

"Easy, General, easy. This may work to your advantage. Ramón Baldez isn't dead. But alive, in your hands, he may be worth much more.''

''But how . . . ?''

''Estaban Vargas wants me to help get him into the country. I think, between us, we can find some way to get Ramón away from the rebels.''

There was a long pause and then a low laugh from the other end of the line. ''As usual, my dear Dominique, your genius is even greater than your beauty.''

''Just have the final half of the money ready to be sent to Switzerland, General.''

She hung up and went straight to her desk. From a top drawer she took a map. She knew every inch of the terrain.

Where would there be a good place for Esteban to bring Ramón ashore?

It took only five minutes to make the decision. It was perfect. The ambush would go completely undetected, and the bodies of Esteban Vargas and his followers would never be found.

FOUR

Nick Carter stepped out of the customs area of Credscencio Rejon Airport into the sultry afternoon air. He stood by the passenger loading door, waiting for the contact to find him.

Eight miles in the distance he saw the heat of the Yucatán rising off the city of Mérida. Somewhere far to his left, on the other side of the peninsula, lay the resort island of Cozumel. There would be brown-skinned, bikini-clad bodies on the beaches, cool rum drinks, and a shower.

Of the three, he needed the shower the most. And a razor.

He'd been in the mountain jungles of Guatemala for three weeks, living off the land and moving from village to village. His cover was as a Peace Corps observer. It didn't hold water, but then the natives didn't give a damn. They were used to American spies, and, in most places, welcomed them. The gringo spies paid the most money for information, true or not.

On the whole, the mission was a flop.

President Baldez refused to get too cozy with the U.S. He had shut a lot of information off, and there was word that he might be cozying up to the rebels. Carter was supposed to dig and find out which way the wind was blowing.

He had made some contacts that were worthwhile,

but all in all, after nearly a month out of circulation, he had learned nothing substantial. His efforts to locate the rebel leader, Esteban Vargas, had been equally fruitless.

Then he had checked in for the first time. The message was no-nonsense, clear, and precise. He was summoned to Mexico, a meeting in the Yucatán, and he was expected an hour ago.

He dropped everything and rattled posthaste down a mountain in a four-wheel-drive jeep back to civilization.

That had been five hours ago. Now, looking like a peasant field hand dressed in baggy white trousers and overblouse, straw hat and backpack, he was in the Yucatán.

When he felt a light tap at his elbow, he looked down at what seemed to be a slim, boyish figure.

"Señor Carter?"

He nodded and stepped back. It was no boy. The breasts in the tight T-shirt were small, but the nipples told the story. The rest of her was in white jeans and a pair of dirty sneakers.

He could swear she wasn't over sixteen.

"Estrella?"

She nodded. "Estrella Gomez. I almost overlooked you. Good disguise."

"No disguise. I've been out of it for almost a month. What's up?"

"They don't tell me. I just run a safe house and a small network. Shall we go?"

She grabbed his arm and guided him to the parking lot and an open jeep. Carter threw his backpack in the rear and grasped the roll bar to get in.

He started to make conversation as the jeep roared to life, but gave up as she flew out of the parking lot. In minutes they were in the country and the whistling of the wind around his ears made conversation impossible. All he could do was grip the roll bar and watch the scenery fly by.

The little lady drove as if she were in the Baja Run and every precious second counted. One small hand held the steering wheel steady while the other worked the gear shift with precision.

"Do you always drive like this?" he shouted above the roar of the engine.

"Always," she shouted back. "Down here on the roads, offense is the best form of defense."

Rarely using the brake, letting the engine work for her, she shot through and around what traffic there was.

They screeched down a straight stretch of road that led toward a mountain and a lot of curves. Then they were twisting up the mountain, passing buses and cars with the jeep's engine whining under the acceleration.

Speeding by a pickup truck loaded with farm workers, Estrella downshifted and jammed the accelerator to the floor. Out in front of the truck she suddenly stood on the brakes. At the same time, she threw the wheel to the left and drifted the jeep into what looked like a solid wall of jungle.

Miraculously, they went through it and emerged on an even narrower lane that went straight up. Over his shoulder he saw the farm workers applauding her prowess with the machine.

Carter felt airsick.

At the top of the mountain she swung the wheel again and they shot through an open gate connected to a tall adobe wall. The gate must have been electrified because it swung closed just as they cleared.

They slid to a halt on the cobbles of a tree-shaded courtyard, and Estrella jumped out.

Carter got out slowly, letting his stomach settle.

"Something wrong?"

"Oh, hell, no. I'm always this color."

He followed her into the house. It was small, dirty adobe on the outside, but well furnished, clean, and neat as a pin on the inside. They were in the large, main room. Down a hall Carter saw two doors, probably bedrooms. In the rear was a kitchen and a small dining room that led out to a sun porch and a pool beyond.

"Jesus, a pool," Carter groaned, already drawn by its shimmering coolness.

"They won't be here until after dark. We've time for a dip if you like."

"I like," he said, nodding.

She opened a closet door and rummaged. "Also a drink and some food. Do me a favor?"

"Sure."

She handed him a towel. "There's a shower by the pool. Take one before you dive in."

Carter chuckled. "Do I smell that bad?"

"Worse. I'll take that."

She grabbed his backpack and headed down the hall. Carter headed toward the rear, shucking clothes as he went.

No shower had ever felt better. It took him the better part of a half hour to get a week's grubbiness from his body. The last time he had bathed had been in an icy mountain stream, so the combination of warmth and soap was like manna from heaven.

He stepped from the stall shaking water from his beard and hair like a shaggy dog.

"There's a cold beer there on the table beside you."

She was standing in the shallow end of the pool with the water hitting her about mid-thigh. And she was stark naked, her hands at her hair, pinning it up.

"I thought I'd join you for a swim," she announced with a smile.

"I can see that," Carter said, dropping the towel from around his waist and hoisting the beer. He drained it and dived in.

They did laps, side by side, for nearly twenty minutes.

"Enough," she panted.

"I'll take a couple more," Carter replied, feeling the pool suck the jungle grime from his pores.

When he pulled himself out, she was standing on the side, wrapped in a large terry towel and holding one for him.

"Like something a little stronger than beer?"

"Sure."

"Tequila?"

"Scotch, neat, if you have it."

"Coming right up."

The air was turning cool, so they moved to the living room, which afforded them a view of the hills but offered protection from the wind. As they downed a couple of drinks, Carter kept glancing at her petite figure in the towel. After all, it had been a month.

She didn't miss the looks.

"Thinking of mixing business with pleasure?" she said, her dark, elfin face breaking into a wide grin.

"The thought was crossing my mind."

"Sorry," she said and shrugged, "I'm afraid we don't have the time."

She moved to a nearby table and returned with a stack of message memos and classified reports.

"You're to brief yourself with these before Hawk and the others get here. You can read while I perform culinary magic."

At the moment, Carter was still more interested in the magic under the towel.

But that mood changed halfway down the first page of the first report. One hell of a lot had happened since he had taken off into the Central American jungle.

It was a good, well-conceived plan. Ramón Baldez had been driven from Paris to Marseille, where he had been spirited aboard a chartered cargo flight to Caracas. From there a small private plane had ferried them to Belize.

Throughout the trip he had been bombarded by all three of his captors with facts, figures, and speculations. He was told that, prior to his father's sudden illness, the old man had met several times with Esteban Vargas to finalize a peace between the rebels and the government.

By the time they crossed the border into their own country and Ramón had met the rebel chieftain in person, the younger Baldez was ninety percent certain that what the men had told him was the truth.

His enemy wasn't Vargas and his mountain rebels. The real danger to the government and Ramón Baldez was from General Emilio Cordovan.

"We have a safe place to hide you, Ramón," Vargas told him. "In the weeks ahead, you will see that, rather than harm you, we want to see you as the next president."

They had crossed the frontier on foot, then transferred to five jeeps and headed toward the safety of the mountains.

By dark they had abandoned their vehicles, and now walked in a single long line with Esteban Vargas in the lead.

They were still about twenty miles from the camp, when the night sky suddenly reverberated with the steady *thwack*, *thwack*, *thwack* of helicopter blades.

Seconds later the long line of men was completely il-
luminated in the glare of powerful searchlights.

Esteban Vargas himself was the first to die, his body
cut nearly in half by machine gun bullets.

Ramón Baldez, unarmed, dived for the darkness of
the heavy brush beside the trail.

Behind him he heard the rebel guns answer the fire
from the helicopters. Nearby he could hear a booming
voice on a bull horn directing the attack. Equally as
loud were the screams of dying men.

Then one sentence from the man on the bull horn
froze Baldez in his tracks. "Be careful of your fire! We
want Baldez alive!"

Seconds later he was surrounded by armed men.
Their leader, a young lieutenant, recognized him at
once.

"General!" he barked into a walkie-talkie.

"Yes?"

"We have Baldez!"

"Bring him to the helicopter."

Baldez was shoved and dragged through the trees to a
wide, brightly lit clearing where three helicopters were
waiting. Near one of them he recognized Army Chief of
Staff Emilio Cordovan.

"Welcome back to your country, Ramón."

If the young man had entertained any thoughts that
he was being rescued, they were quickly dispelled.

"General, we have three prisoners."

"And the others?"

"All dead, General."

"Good. Bury them deeply. I want no trace."

The three frightened rebel prisoners were shoved into
the light, and empty guns were placed in their hands.
Ramón Baldez, his hands handcuffed before him, was
posed on his knees before them. A newspaper bearing

the current day's date was stretched across his chest. Several photos were taken, and then Baldez was hoisted into one of the helicopters.

The last thing he saw before the machine lifted was the execution of the three remaining rebel prisoners.

There was barely a mumbled hello from the head of AXE, David Hawk, as he and his entourage passed Carter at the door and arranged themselves around the large dining room table.

There was a short, bespectacled man with a receding hairline that had reached the top of his head. Carter had met him a few times before. His name was John Fuller, and he was in the Central American section of the State Department.

Besides Hawk's two bodyguards, Carter also recognized Louis Hodent, head of Interpol Central in Paris.

Carter quickly shook hands all around and moved into the empty chair at the table.

"You've read the reports, Nick?"

"I have, but I must say I don't completely understand them. It sounds as though the rebel, Vargas, is making a last-ditch move to take over the country, but that doesn't fit with what I've been able to learn being down there the last month."

David Hawk growled around his cigar and nodded to Louis Hodent. The big cop rolled his eyes one more time over the reports and looked up at Carter.

"Ambassador Alvarez was killed with his secretary, Milena Silvado, at his summer lakefront house in Maryland. We've had to do a lot of data collecting from various police agencies, but we think we have an ID on the killer."

"I would like to interject," said Fuller for the State

Department, "that the bodies were found *in flagrante delicto*."

"In other words," Carter replied dryly, "Alvarez was banging her when he bought it."

"Exactly." Fuller coughed. "Milena Silvado was a married woman. The papers, both in Washington and Guatemala City, are having a field day with it. And even though President Baldez is dying, it is having its effect on his administration."

Carter nodded and turned back to Louis Hodent. "Who do you have an ID on as the killer?"

"Getting to that. They were both shot with a high-powered rifle, probably an American 30.06. The gun hasn't been found. We got a description from a motel clerk and a gas station attendant. We also found an abandoned Ford with Montreal plates at Dulles Airport. The description matches a man who took a TWA flight that night to Portugal."

"Anything in Lisbon?"

"Nothing, but it looks like he didn't stay very long. He chartered a flight to Marbella. Twenty-four hours later he checked into an inn at the foot of the Sierra de Cazorla mountains north of Granada."

"And Alfredo Diaz was killed in a chalet in the Sierras."

"Exactly. We found a Russian Stechkin, clean, no prints, beside the bed. But by this time we didn't need prints. The killer is the same. He was traveling under a forged Guatemalan passport in the name of Raul Santiago, but his description fits this man to a T."

Carter glanced down at the photograph and groaned. "Benito Venezzio? But he's dead . . ."

"He's *supposed* to be dead. We have run complete questionnaires through the military and the police down there. Supposedly his car ran off a mountain and burst into flames. The authorities claim that even though the body was badly burned it could still be identified. They have assured us that Venezzio is dead."

"But three people identified him as very much alive," Carter replied.

Hodent nodded and jabbed a finger at the photograph. "They identified that. The motel woman in Maryland was emphatic. She doesn't like Latins. The gas station owner remembers him because he paid with a fifty. A waitress will never forget him. She fell in love on the spot. Ditto a maid in Spain. He bedded her."

Carter shook his head and lit a cigarette as he skimmed the written version of what Hodent had just told him.

Finally the Killmaster slammed the table. "Okay, the guy's alive and killing people. But two things I don't understand. Venezzio was not only Esteban Vargas's best friend, he was also his best hatchet man. If Benito Venezzio is doing this killing, he's doing it on Vargas's orders."

"That's what we figure," Hawk growled.

"Number two," Carter said, leaning back in his chair, "I know Venezzio, at least by reputation. He's a pro. He doesn't make mistakes. He would never let himself be made like this. For God's sake, this guy has left a trail halfway around the world!"

The three men listened in silence until Carter was done and then exchanged guarded looks. Then David Hawk cranked up his moldy cigar and took the floor.

"You were sent down there, Nick, to find out the true stability of Baldez's government. Also, you were supposed to find out if there was any truth that he was starting to play games with the rebels."

"And that I did," Carter replied. "Esteban Vargas has just about had it. I'm sure he was ready to talk turkey with Baldez. There's no reason for him to kill Alvarez and Diaz."

"Would you say Baldez's government is stable?"

"I would," Carter stated.

"And if he dies?"

Carter thought for a moment. "His son, Ramón. I'm sure the younger Baldez would be a replica of the father and carry on his reforms."

Hawk almost managed a smile.

"Ramón Baldez was kidnapped in Paris by four men in a Fiat. Shots were exchanged. By whom, we don't know. But the Fiat was found with a very large bullet hole in the right rear door."

"Where was the car when they found it?"

"A private airstrip near Marseille. We think Ramón was taken back to Guatemala."

"By whom?" Carter asked.

"Vargas and his rebels."

"Can you be sure of that?"

"Reasonably," Hawk replied. "One of the four men was shot and left dead on the Rue St. Blanc. His name was Jesus Miranda. He was not only Esteban Vargas's cousin, he was also the man's second in command after Venezzio was killed."

Carter let the air out of his lungs with an audible *whoosh*. "Vargas must have gone mad." And then he was suddenly on his feet. He began pacing, going over in his mind all that it had absorbed in the two hours since Hawk and the group had arrived.

"There is another possibility," he said at last.

"Let's hear it," Hawk growled.

"General Emilio Cordovan. With Alvarez and Diaz

out of the way and President Baldez dead, Ramón is the only person who could stop Cordovan from taking over the country.''

All three of the men still sitting at the table were now smiling.

"We had thought of that,'' Hawk said. "But in any event, whoever has Ramón Baldez, we want him back.''

Suddenly the AXE chief's hands dived into his briefcase and came out with a thick manila envelope.

"In here, Nick, are the names of a neutral team. Needless to say, we can't get involved. You know all these men. I want you to put them together and find Ramón Baldez. There is also a female contact in Guatemala. She is trusted by Baldez—''

He was interrupted by auto tires sliding to a halt on the gravel outside. Seconds later there was a rap at the door. It opened a crack, and Estrella Gomez's dark head peeped through.

"Urgent . . . from Mexico City.''

Hawk rose and lumbered from the room.

Louis Hodent leaned toward Carter. "There are one or two more items concerning Alfredo Diaz's death in Spain. They might not be important . . .''

"Shoot. I'll take all I can get.''

"Before he died, Diaz made a call to Ramón Baldez at the Château Boulange in Fontainebleau. We don't know what was said, but . . .''

"Diaz could have set the president's son up for the kidnap.''

"It's possible,'' Hodent admitted. "One other thing . . .''

"Yeah?''

"There was definitely a woman in the chalet with Diaz before he was shot.''

"You're sure?''

Hodent smiled. "Nick, I am French."

"You'll keep me informed through Hawk of anything new?"

"Of course."

Hawk came back into the room like an overheated steam engine. "Gentlemen, if you would be so kind as to leave me alone with Carter."

Fuller and Hodent left quickly. Hawk had that effect of command. The two bodyguards were like machines: hear no, see no, speak no. They remained by the door.

The Killmaster knew that whatever the message from Mexico City was, it was important . . . and probably not good news.

"I think our decision has been made for us, Nick," the AXE chief said, sliding the thick manila envelope across the table. To it he added an eight-by-ten glossy photo. "The one kneeling is Ramón Baldez. The three in fatigues with the rifles standing around them are part of Esteban Vargas's rebel army. We've identified them from our own intelligence files."

Carter examined the picture and the brief dispatch. "Shit," he hissed. "Any demands?"

"Forthcoming," Hawk replied, tapping the manila envelope. "Time to go to work, Nick."

Carter reached for the envelope and paused. "Give me seventy-two hours."

"What?"

"Seventy-two hours. I didn't accomplish much down there in the last month, but I came up with one lead to Vargas. His ex-wife has changed her name. She's a singer, owns her own club in a little town on the island of Aruba."

"What's she got to do with it?" Hawk asked, frowning.

"She and Vargas had a pretty messy split, but she still

believes in the cause and helps Vargas. I think if anyone could get me to him, it's her.''

"What can you accomplish alone, even if you do get to him?''

"I can talk to him. If he does have Ramón Baldez, maybe I can convince him to give him up. Also, by facing him I can get his side of the story, maybe the truth from the horse's mouth.''

"It's a chance,'' Hawk said, grinding on his cigar, "and it would save a lot of problems. Okay, seventy-two hours. But, Nick . . .''

"Yeah?''

"That's it. Then it's back here to get the envelope.''

"You're on. Can I take this?'' He picked up the photo of Baldez and his captors.

"If you think it'll help.''

"See you in three days.''

He instructed Estrella to book him on any flight that would connect him fast to Aruba. In his room, he re-packed his backpack and met her at the jeep.

"There's a commercial flight to Maracaibo in an hour. You can pick up a charter from there to Aruba.''

"Can we make it?''

"If we hurry.''

"Then hurry. This time I don't care how much you scare the hell out of me.''

She broke her record to the airport and walked him to the boarding gate.

"You're taking care of an envelope for me, but I hope I won't need it.''

She had to go clear to her toes to get her arms around his neck, but she managed. She might have looked like a little girl, but the way she used her lips and tongue was all woman.

"If you don't need the envelope, does that mean I won't see you again?"

"Oh, you'll see me again," Carter said, gently running his hand over her round bottom. "You can make book on it."

Fifteen minutes later he was heading south to find a woman who now called herself Lorena del Mar.

FIVE

Lupe Vargas aka Lorena del Mar hadn't exactly risen to high-roller heights since leaving her husband and her native land. The Casa del Mar club was in a small village near the center of the island. The village was poor, and so were the inhabitants who were its only customers.

Carter got directions from the girl at the auto rental counter, and took off. It took him the better part of an hour to find the village, and just a few minutes to pull up in front of a cellar joint with a paint-peeling sign above: CASA DEL MAR.

The building above the cellar was early Spanish crumbling, and the paint on the window moldings was peeling more than the sign.

He pulled the keys but didn't lock the car. He figured his timing was perfect. It was just a few minutes before two in the morning. The club would probably have already emptied out and would be about to close.

Carter had one foot on the curb when something big, wide, and dark with an ugly knife scar on his left cheek stepped from the shadows.

"You can't park here. You'll have to—"

"Take care of my car, will you?" Carter said, pressing the big man's flesh with an American twenty.

He brought it up to his face as if he were going to bite it. When he saw the denomination, his teeth became neon.

"No pussy in there—all gone home."

"That's okay. I'm doing without tonight." Carter went down three steps into a dim foyer.

There was a languid, sloe-eyed child-woman behind a counter counting money out of a cigar box. She looked thirty, but probably registered in around sixteen. She looked up quickly as Carter approached.

"Entertainment is over. We're closing."

"That's okay. I just want a drink."

"That's be five dollars."

"For what?"

"Cover charge for the entertainment."

"You just said the entertainment's over."

"It is, but we still charge."

He gave her a ten. "Keep the change."

Her smile changed her face but not much. It had a frozen, tailored quality and her heavily penciled eyebrows arched upward when she saw the bill.

The bill disappeared down the front of her blouse and her eyes took a harder look at this handsome American with money. They began to glow and the tailored quality vanished from her smile. She leaned forward so the counter pushed lush breasts up even more revealingly above the scooped neckline of her blouse.

"You can tell me something I need to know," he said, twisting another ten between his fingers.

"I'm through in a half hour."

She had long, smooth fingers with nails lacquered ruby red. The tips were warm and they pulsed against his hand as they took the bill. Carter leaned one elbow on the counter and studied the interior decorations of the thin blouse with appreciation.

"I might be very interested . . . in a half hour. Right now I need to know if the lady is still inside."

She wriggled a trifle and moved closer, bathing him

with body warmth and cheap perfume. "You'll get a lot further with me."

"I'll keep that in mind," he said, trailing the tips of his fingers across her bare forearm and letting his smile widen into a grin.

"Besides, only Reno shares her bed. And Reno's bad."

Carter lifted his gaze slowly, catching the smooth line of her throat, the pouting mouth that was close to his with the wet tip of tongue just inside, the dark eyes that opened a little wider as he met them and glowed with open invitation.

"Bed is not what I want from the lady," he said. "Is she still here?"

"She's always here. She lives upstairs."

The come-hither light went out of her eyes and Carter entered the main room of the club.

It was typical. Long, narrow, and dark. Once-red paper on the walls was now a smoky gray. Ditto for the cloths on the round tables. The smell was beer and perfume, and the music from a jukebox was Herb Alpert.

Sweet simplicity for the hometown boys and the cheaper grade of tourist.

Carter turned into the deserted bar, and a beefy bartender came alive from his trance over polishing a glass.

"It is last call, mister."

"Then I'll call for a scotch, neat."

It came in a heavy glass thimble that cost him four bucks. Carter carefully gathered up the buck left from a five and pocketed it. He smiled gently at the glowering look this action got him from the bartender.

"Is the lady upstairs?" Carter asked, sipping the whiskey.

The bartender rested a chunky forearm on the bar

and blinked his hooded eyes. "What cheapskate is asking?"

Carter fingered a five from his breast pocket and slid it across the bar. "This one."

"You sound American."

"I am."

The bill came back at him. "The lady don't talk to Americans."

"She'll talk to me," Carter said.

"Fuck you, buddy."

Carter didn't say anything. He carefully rolled the whiskey around in his glass for a moment, then threw it in the man's beefy face.

The barman ducked and sputtered, swiping at his face with a bar rag and stooping to reach for something.

Carter didn't alter his casual posture. "I wouldn't," he said, and something in his voice jerked the man to a halt before he straightened up.

Their eyes locked across the bar, and the chill, icelike quality of Carter's drilled into the veined milkiness of the other's.

"I would like a few words with the lady," Carter said, his voice like a smooth stone.

"Trouble, Emanuel?"

The voice came from behind Carter's right shoulder. He turned casually. A man had emerged from the dimness of the rear. He wasn't big like the barman. He didn't even look tough. But in the half-light from behind the bar he exuded menace. Maybe it was his eyes.

His hair was slick and black. A slight figure and a boyish face. All but the eyes. They weren't boyish. They weren't anything you could describe. Holes for him to see through. Mirroring nothing. No imagination, no feelings. Nothing.

He stood hard on the heels of two-toned boots, hands thrust deep in the slanting pockets of a tan sports jacket. He could be holding a pocket gun. At any rate, Carter caught the bulge of a shoulder rig that the carefully tailored jacket had been built to hide.

"Bastard got nasty at me," the bartender sputtered. "You want me to—"

"Shut up." The man's voice was like his eyes: flat and devoid of expression yet somehow imbued with the reptilian menace of a Gila monster. He didn't look at the bartender as he spoke. He asked Carter, "Why?"

Carter shrugged. He was leaning sideways with one elbow on the bar. "You must be Reno."

"I am. And you?"

"The man who wants a few words with your partner."

The trace of a smile appeared on the man's face. "Whoever you are, you got balls."

His right hand started to move. It had only gone a few inches when Carter flexed his right forearm muscle. The tension activated the spring release in a chamois sheath beneath his shirt. A stiletto that the Killmaster affectionately called Hugo shot into his palm. At the same time his arm shot out.

The point of the stiletto drew a tiny dot of blood on Reno's throat.

"Move that hand another inch and you'll be breathing through a new hole in your throat."

"Enough, Reno!"

Carter looked over Reno's head to the end of the long room. A woman was now standing in the pool of light beside the piano.

She was tall and slender and impossibly lovely. At thirty feet her gaze had an impact that hit Carter square in the gut.

Her hair was long and glossy black, floating down over her shoulders to her hips. Her face was a chiseled mixture of Spanish and Indian hollows and plains, and her eyes were the blackest Carter had ever seen.

"What do you want?" she asked. Her voice had the throaty quality of a saloon singer who had been singing a little too long.

"Talk . . . with you. It won't take long."

Carter dropped the stiletto from Reno's throat and moved away from the bar in her direction.

Reno was in his way and he didn't move. When Carter was close, the other man spoke in a voice that was barely audible. "The other way is out."

Carter paused, wrenching his gaze away from the woman with an effort to look down at the little man. When he spoke, his tone was as soft as Reno's. "I don't have much time, so I'm not going to waste any more of it pissing around with you. Step aside or I'll step over you."

Carter started forward again, and this time Reno moved.

"Another time, son of a bitch," he mumbled as Carter passed him.

The Killmaster paid no more attention to him. He headed for the woman standing in the soft pool of light by the piano.

This woman had the key to the whole situation. Now the trick would be for Carter to convince her to pass it on to him.

As he got closer he noticed her dress and the body it hugged like a second skin. It was as black as her eyes, and swept over her solid curves to the floor.

Carter was close to her now, close enough to smell her perfume. She hadn't moved in all that time. She just stood, her eyes locked to his.

"Lupe Vargas," Carter said in a whisper.

Her only facial reaction was the bare twitch of a carefully shaped eyebrow. "Who are you, gringo?"

He was close enough now to see her face more clearly. It was as hard as it was beautiful, and when she spoke the lips hardly moved. They were thin, coolly perfect lips that had been lightly touched with rose lipstick that hadn't ruined their contour.

"My name is Carter. I want to talk about Esteban Vargas."

He handed her the photograph of Ramón Baldez and the three rebels. Again there was only a bare reaction. Here was a woman in total control of herself.

Carter sensed movement behind him and tensed. "Tell your boyfriend to go away."

"Why should I?" she said, looking up lazily from the picture.

"Because if you don't, I'll kill him."

"Reno . . ."

"*Sí?*"

"Go away." Her eyes smiled at Carter as she said it. He also thought he saw a slight pulse at the base of her throat. "Let us talk . . . privately. I have an apartment upstairs."

She moved away and Carter followed her through a door and up a narrow stairway.

He found his eyes riveted on the movement in front of him. There is something about a woman going on a stairway with a lone man close behind her, something disturbingly intimate.

As he followed her closely on the stairway, his face level with her moving hips in the tight dress, it was difficult to imagine she had ever been in the mountains with a machine gun in ther hands.

They reached the top and, still without a backward glance or a spoken word, she unlocked a door and crossed the threshold.

Carter followed her without hesitation.

It was a woman's room, warm and alive with color and pattern. Blue draperies hung low to the floor from a wide window at the far end. The room was thickly carpeted from wall to wall with a pattern of dull reds and yellows, and not cluttered with furniture.

But it was cluttered with a man's white shirt lying rumpled and conspicuous just inside an open door leading into the bedroom. Reno's shirt. A mute reminder to Carter that he was alone there with another man's woman.

Past the rumpled shirt and through the open door, he could see half an oversize bed with the covers thrown back, one pillow and the sheet wrinkled. Past the bed was a low, glass-topped vanity almost bare on top. Cut-glass stoppered flacons and powder boxes on one side, a large-caliber revolver on the other.

"How did you find me?"

"Bits and pieces," he replied. "I've spent the better part of a month in Guatemala gathering them."

"Have you come to kill me? Are you a CIA assassin?"

Carter passed over his real ID. She scanned it quickly and passed it back. "What do you want?"

"The photograph should answer that. All hell is breaking loose in your country."

"I'm beyond that."

"I don't think so. I think your personal life with Esteban Vargas was a mess, but I don't think you've stopped believing in what he's trying to do."

"Esteban fights a hopeless cause."

"Perhaps, but it will be even more hopeless if that photograph is true. I want to see him. I think you can arrange it."

She stood in the center of the long room facing away from him, her hands hanging limply by her sides. He sensed a hopelessness and uncertainty in her stance.

"I don't want any more to do with it . . . with him, with fighting. I'm tired."

Carter moved to her. He grasped her gently by the shoulder and turned her to face him. Her face was pinched and bloodless, and her breath came fast between tight lips as her breasts rose and fell rapidly.

Carefully, he sat her in a chair and crouched beside her. In slow, measured tones he told her everything he knew.

Her reaction to the assassinations of Alvarez and Diaz was minimal. It was as if she expected it. There was only a slight nodding of the head when she heard of the Paris kidnapping and the theories behind the photograph.

The big reaction came when Carter related all the details he had gotten from the Interpol man, Louis Hodent.

"Venezzio . . . Benito Venezzio?" she whispered.

"That's what it looks like," Carter said. "But I don't have time now to track Venezzio down if he is alive. I need to see Vargas and convince him to give Ramón up if he's got him. That's why I need you."

She sat motionless, but the fingers of both hands began to tighten into fists in her lap. They relaxed and tensed again. Then they were lifted to both sides of her head, fingertips thrusting into her hair.

"What happens if I can't get you to Esteban?"

Carter's teeth, as he stood and moved away from her,

were set so tightly together that his jaws ached. "I've been instructed to put together a neutral team to go in after Baldez. If I do that, there will be no talking. I'll kill anyone who tries to stop me."

She stared at him for a long moment, as though it were the first time she had seen his face. Carter held his breath until she lowered her eyes at last and spoke.

"It will take several hours, many telephone calls. Where are you staying on the island?"

"Nowhere . . . yet."

"Check into the Divi Divi Beach Hotel. It's the closest to here. I'll call you or send word when I know something."

Carter moved toward her across the heavy carpet, his eyes searching her face. When he was close he saw the perspiration wetting her temples, the pulsing tremors in the rounded softness of her throat beneath the lifted chin.

"You will send word."

"I will."

"Because, if you don't, I'll be back."

"I will. Who knows? If I help you and you succeed, I might even be able to go back to my country someday."

Carter moved to the door. Something in her words and the way she had said them made him pause.

"Why Reno?"

"Reno." She thought, and then shrugged. "I had nothing . . . no money, nothing, when I fled Guatemala. I was a revolutionary on the run and I was tired of having nothing. I wanted something. Reno wanted my body. It is a trade."

She stopped talking and Carter opened the door. But before he could close it behind him she spoke again.

"Be careful of Reno. He is very jealous of his possessions, and I can't control him when he is out of my sight. Also, you humiliated him downstairs. He will never forget that."

"Does he know who you really are?"

"No, and he wouldn't care."

All I need, Carter thought, moving down the stairway, *is a battle with a jealous boyfriend.*

SIX

Carter awakened at noon. His first thought was the car that had followed him all the way from the village to the hotel.

It was obviously Reno or one of his people. Carter hadn't tried to lose it. That would have been silly on an island the size of Aruba. Even if he had lost the tail, the Killmaster was pretty sure that a man with Reno's connections would have found him again in no time.

He called the desk and asked for messages. There weren't any. After ordering breakfast, he padded to the bath and a long shower. He was dressing when his breakfast arrived.

Carter studied the waiter. He was a local, no kid, and looked like he knew the underside of the island.

Waiters and bartenders, Carter knew, didn't miss much. And on an island this size they probably didn't miss anything.

"Will there be anything else, sir?"

"No . . . yes, wait." Carter lifted a twenty from his wallet and pressed it into the waiter's hand. "Last night I met a man named Reno."

Two eyebrows went up and two dark eyes started darting all over the room. Carter had hit a nerve. He just hoped the waiter knew Reno and was neutral.

The man's eyes stopped roaming long enough to look

at the twenty and back up at Carter. The Killmaster added a mate to the bill.

"Reno Poppi, Venezuela man, very dangerous. He buys certain products in Colombia, transports them across Venezuela, and holds them in Aruba until the price is right in the Bahamas. You understand?"

"I understand," Carter said, nodding. "Does Reno Poppi have a lot of friends?"

The waiter smiled. "Here, on the island, I would say five, maybe six."

Carter smiled. Six and Poppi he could handle.

The Killmaster ate and killed the afternoon in his room. By dusk he was getting antsy.

At the desk he checked again. There were still no messages. He called Washington from a pay phone in the lobby. He had already wasted twenty-four of his seventy-two hours, and Ginger Bateman, David Hawk's right hand at AXE, didn't fail to inform him of it.

"You think I don't know how minor a jealous boyfriend is right now?" Carter growled. "What's the latest word down south?"

"Confusion," Ginger replied. "State's advice was to keep everything quiet. General Cordovan agreed, but somehow everything that has happened has gotten leaked to the press. Vargas has made some demands."

"Like what?"

"Ten million dollars in cash paid into a special account, and safe conduct out of the country for himself and his people. General Cordovan has vowed publicly that he'll wipe out every rebel in the country before he'll pay it."

"That sounds like the general," Carter hissed. "Any difference in the old man's condition?"

"None. President Baldez is hanging on, but by a thread. Hawk says this thing with Ramón must be settled before his father dies or it's a powder keg. State would have to recognize Cordovan as head of the government, like it or not, just to avert a bloody civil war."

"I'm working on it."

Carter hung up and headed for the bar. Halfway there he was intercepted by a bellboy. "Mr. Carter?"

"Yes."

"This message was just delivered to the desk."

Carter lifted the envelope from the boy's tray and dropped a bill on it. "In person?"

"No, sir. By phone."

"Thanks."

It was simple and to the point: *Call 741-291*.

He beelined back to the phone booth and dialed the number. A woman answered.

"This is Carter."

"This is Amalia Persevez."

"Terrific," he growled. "Who's Amalia Persevez?"

"You don't remember me. I saw you last night at the Casa del Mar."

Carter remembered the bosomy cover-charge girl. "What is it?"

"Lorena told me to call you. I am to meet you and take you to her."

It smelled, but so far it was the only contact he had and he had no way of checking it.

"All right," he said. "Are you coming to the hotel?"

"No, you are being watched by two of Reno's men. Lose them and I will meet you in an hour, after dark."

"Where?"

"Two miles north of the hotel is a private fishing pier. I will meet you there, at the wall above the breakwater."

The line went dead in Carter's ear. He hung up the phone and rolled his eyes around the lobby.

It wasn't hard spotting them among the tourists.

There were two, overdressed and trying their damnedest to look inconspicuous.

In the hotel lobby, they looked like a couple of pimps at the Vatican.

The Killmaster returned to his room, changed clothes, and checked out of the hotel. The two were on him as he put his bag in the car. He also spotted a third in a Cadillac sedan half a block away on the opposite side of the street.

It was about two miles from the hotel to the beach resort of Oranjestad. By the time he reached the center of the town he was leading a caravan, with the two pimps in an old Chevrolet trailing close and the Cadillac bringing up the rear.

He parked near the center of town and began the routine.

In a phone booth he talked gibberish for five minutes, walked a block to another booth and called the airport. It took a page nearly five minutes to reach the charter pilot who had flown him from Caracas. Carter had had him on hold since they had landed.

He was a rough guy from Houston, Texas, who had come to the Caribbean to run away from a nagging wife and a few hundred nagging creditors.

"Bill, this is Carter."

"Yeah."

"I take it you're ready to roll?"

"Man, I been ready to roll since we landed. This place is the pits."

"We leave tonight."

"Good, I'm tired of sitting around with my thumb up my ass."

"You're getting paid for it."

"Excellent point. I'll file a flight plan for Caracas for the return. We can leave the minute you get here."

"Do that, except your first leg will be near the Vago Chico, in Belize."

A chuckle. "Bet you don't want a flight plan for that leg filed."

"No. Any problem with that?"

"Only if you got dope on you when we land."

"No way."

"Then you pay, I fly."

Carter hung up and started walking. It was a clear routine. He cut across a park, through a bar, and out the back. Then he doubled back and pulled the same routine in another area.

If it had been cops following him, it would have been termed open surveillance. They didn't try to hide the tail at all.

And after twenty minutes, Carter knew that they could have tailed him to the moon if they had wanted to.

But by the time he stole a motor scooter and headed back out the beach road, there was no sight of them.

He had barely turned off the highway when he spotted the fishing pier. That was his second warning. The first had been the tail itself.

The girl was standing alone at the top of the steps above the seawall. Carter parked the scooter and joined her. She was dressed in a sweater that did wonderful things to her chest, and a skirt that left nothing beneath it to the imagination.

But Carter was more interested in the way her hands worried her purse and the way she danced her weight from foot to foot, as if she were about to pee her pants.

"Hi," he said, clutching her elbow.

"Hello . . . you're late."

"Yeah, I had a hard time getting rid of the company. Where is she?"

"There, in that boat at the end of the pier."

Carter smiled. "She needed you to lead me two hundred feet down a pier to a boat?"

"She, uh . . . she didn't want to show herself."

"I see. Well, lead the way."

By now he knew it was a setup. But he made one small miscalculation. He figured they would try for him on the boat.

She was walking slowly in front of him. Ahead lay the gate in the wall leading down to the pier. She was just through it when she turned and reached for his hands.

Behind him, Carter heard a soft footstep and a muffled grunt. A millisecond later, a billy whipped into his kidney and the Killmaster buckled to the side, raising his arms to protect his head.

The billy brushed his hair, barely missing.

As Carter hit the ground and tried to roll, he saw the big black who had been driving the Cadillac. Evidently he had been crouching in the darkness beside the wall.

The toe of a hard boot found the Killmaster's gut. He doubled tightly to regroup. The boot kept kicking, landing on his arms. From the first hit in the kidneys, Carter's legs seemed to have come unhinged.

He rolled hard into the black's legs as the man tried to bring the billy down across his shoulder. It worked, somewhat.

The billy missed, but the guy was as agile as an acrobat. He regained his balance and got another good kick in with his boot, dead square where Carter's ribs joined his stomach.

He was taking a licking, but he was also learning.

Reno Poppi didn't know who he really was, didn't know the whole story. He probably just figured Carter was some dude out to take his woman. He had probably given his boys the order to just give Carter a beating.

That was Reno Poppi's mistake.

The black's boot started far back and swung viciously at Carter's groin. It was the kick he expected, and avoided it easily by rolling and coming up on one knee.

The big man followed up with the billy to Carter's throat. The Killmaster ducked under the blow and blocked it with his forearm. At the same time, he let the other man's weight cover him and rolled to his back.

The man went on over Carter's head and landed flat on his back. Carter was on him in an instant, his forearms closed over his throat.

He only meant to black him out, but the fear of defeat made the man go for broke. He slipped a knife from his belt and brought it into position for a thrust at Carter's side.

It never landed, but it served to unseat the Killmaster and separate them.

"Drop it or die," Carter hissed.

The black came for him. Carter stepped through the thrust and his left foot exploded into the man's chest, shattering his sternum. He landed on his back, blood pouring from both sides of his mouth.

It would be a slow, painful death, taking at least an hour.

Carter stepped forward, bringing the side of his hand in an upward motion under the man's nostrils. It was a crushing blow that sent splinters of bone directly into the brain.

There was hardly any sound as the bulky body slid down the steps, teetered on the edge of the pier, and made a dull splash into the water.

Panting, holding his aching side, Carter turned to where the girl stood. She hadn't moved an inch since it had begun. Her mouth was drooping, and all he could see were the whites of her eyes.

"Where are the other two?" he said, grasping her by the shoulder. "The ones in the fancy suits driving the Chevrolet?"

"Help him," she gasped.

"Help who?"

"Ezan, him. He'll drown."

"He's already dead."

Then she screamed.

Carter had no time for hysterics. He forced her down to the pier, still screaming. Then he upended her and, holding her by the ankles, dipped her up and down in the water until the screaming stopped.

"Where are the other two!"

"All right," she choked. "Not here—back at the club."

"You mean they just sent *him*?"

"Ezan has never lost a fight. He is the meanest and best on the island."

"Well, he lost his last fight tonight. Where is she?"

Silence . . . for two long dunkings, and then a sputtering answer.

"An apartment . . . one of Reno's on the other side of the island, in Bushiribana."

"Truth?"

"I swear," she gasped.

Carter hauled her up and dragged her to the other side of the pier. He grabbed a handful of her hair and held her head over the side. The black's body floated just beneath her eyes.

"It had better be the truth, or you'll be floating off a pier in Bushiribana just like that."

"It is truth, I swear! I must do what Reno tells me or he will beat me!"

"From now on," Carter whispered directly into her ear, "you do what *I* tell you. Because, lady, I won't beat you up, I'll kill you . . . and you can make book on it. You have a car?"

"Yes . . . up there."

"Let's go. You can tell me all the details on the way across the island!"

General Emilio Cordovan snatched the phone from its cradle before the first ring had ended. "Yes!"

"It's me. What is it?"

"I just got a call from one of my business associates in Aruba. An American has been trying to make contact with the Vargas woman."

"So, why do you call me?"

"My dear Dominique, you are playing every side against the middle. His name is Carter, Nick Carter. What do you know of him?"

"Nothing. I have never heard the name."

"Are you sure?"

"The Americans have not contacted me."

"Reno Poppi seems to think this Carter is an agent. He heard over the microphone in the Vargas woman's apartment that Carter wants to talk to Esteban. Surely you know something about this, Dominique."

"I don't, I swear it. Besides, Reno Poppi is yours. I want no part of his kind. You set him up with the Vargas woman. If the Americans have found her, it is your problem. I told you she should have been eliminated long ago."

"Yes, Dominique, you did. And with Esteban dead, she can offer us no more intelligence. I'll have it taken care of right away."

"And, General, while I have you on the line, may I say that what you are doing is mad!"

"How is that, my dear?"

"Don't think I don't know what you are doing, and don't think for a moment that if anything goes wrong, the Americans won't know. I didn't hand Ramón Baldez to you as a pawn."

"I don't know what you mean, Dominique."

"Bullshit. He should be killed. Instead, you will ransom him from your own men for ten million dollars."

"Dominique, that was your fee for you and your friends' help. How do you care how you are paid?"

"I care because of the Americans. When you are in power you can rape the country. How you do it is not my concern. One sixth of the American aid alone for one year will pay our fee. I say that by trying this subterfuge with Ramón Baldez, you are endangering our entire plan. What do you plan on doing with Ramón after he is ransomed?"

"I will keep him sequestered, of course. And then, when he makes his first public appearance, I thought perhaps our friend Venezzio could make one more appearance."

"No! No, Emilio, don't! Benito's work is done. Mine will soon be finished. Then I disappear, as he has already done. Then I want no more to do with you or the country."

"Very well. I will handle Ramón in my own fashion. You have nothing to fear, Dominique. A deal is a deal. I gain a country and you regain your former wealth. I will have the Vargas woman eliminated tonight. Thanks to you, I know the location of the rest of the rebel camps. In a few days' time they will be wiped out. Good night, Dominique."

"Good night, General."

He used his thumb to make the disconnect, and dialed another number. As it rang he chuckled to himself. The phone in his hand was probably the only official phone in the country that wasn't bugged.

"Yes?"

"Reno, I think it best you end your sordid romance with the woman."

"I'll take care of it. Also, I have the dates of the next shipment into Guatemala City."

"Reno, how many times must I tell you, I don't have time to handle such trivia. You have Eduardo's private number?"

"Of course, General. And, about the woman . . . I'll handle it tonight."

"And the American, Reno . . . make sure he leaves Aruba thinking you are only a jealous suitor."

"That is being taken care of."

"Good night, Reno."

"Good night, General."

Emilio Cordovan made one more phone call before retiring.

"Eduardo?"

"Yes, General?"

"Reno will be calling you shortly with the date and times of the next shipment through Guatemala City."

"*Si.*"

"I think that will be the last shipment, Eduardo. Reno Poppi and his business has served us well, but I think it will be too risky to continue when I am president."

"Yes, General. But Poppi could be very difficult . . ."

"I've thought of that. Do we have anyone we could send to Aruba?"

"I believe so. I will take care of it."

"Thank you, Eduardo. Good night."

"Good night, General."

Emilio Cordovan hung up the receiver, hoisted his bulk from the chair, and walked into his bedroom.

They were there, waiting, the lovers, the boy and the girl, both very young and very beautiful.

Emilio Cordovan eased his huge bulk into a chair and smiled at them.

"Begin," he said, and settled back to enjoy the evening's entertainment.

SEVEN

It was an interesting story little Amalia Persevez told as they drove across the island. But puzzling.

She had been taken off the streets by Reno Poppi about a year before to work in the club. But her main job was to stay close to Lorena del Mar as much as possible. She was to report back to Reno the name of anyone to whom Lorena spoke and whatever conversation she overheard.

Also, in the guise of being Lorena's friend, Amalia had taken messages to a fisherman in Sint Nicolaas. Always these messages were taken to Reno Poppi first.

Amalia claimed that setting Carter up was the first time Poppi had ordered her to do anything beyond her spying on the lady.

Carter believed her. He also decided, through some intricate questioning, that she did not know who Lorena really was.

But now he wasn't so sure that Reno Poppi didn't know the real identity of his mistress. All the spying was just a little too much for a jealous lover.

"What will you do with me?" Amalia whined as Carter guided the car through the outskirts of Bushiribana.

"Depends."

"On what?"

"On how much of what you've told me is the truth."

"It is, I swear—"

"Which way?" Carter barked, cutting her off.

"Right. It's three buildings down . . . there!"

Carter braked to the curb and killed the engine. Even though it was still early in the evening, there was very little activity in the area. Most of the lights and noise was blocks away, nearer the beach.

The houses along the block were three-story crumbling whitewashed tenements. It was an area where the local domestics, bartenders, and general workers who manned the beach resorts lived.

"Which floor?"

"The top one. They are floor-through flats, three rooms. The bedroom's in the rear."

"How do you know she'll be in the bedroom?"

Carter had thought it impossible for the girl's face to redden, but it did.

"I heard Reno tell Emanuel that he and Chico could have her before . . ."

"Before what?"

"I don't know. Reno said 'ship her out,' or something like that."

Carter nodded, his face a grim mask. He had a pretty good idea what Reno meant. It was obvious now that the little hood knew a lot more about his lover than she'd thought.

He got out of the car, pulling the girl behind him. In the rear, he unlocked the trunk. "Get in!"

"I'll suffocate . . ."

"Not for a while."

"But what if you don't come back?"

"You'd just better hope I do."

He slammed the trunk lid, shutting off her whines, and moved toward the second building in the block. Each of the buildings was about three feet apart and connected by a narrow, rusty fire escape.

The small lobby was deserted. Carter went quickly up two flights of stairs to the third floor. The higher he rose, the stronger the aroma of frying fish filled his nostrils.

He walked down a dimly lit hallway toward the window that led out onto the fire escape.

A door opened just to his left and a head, the hair in enormous pink foam curlers, appeared. She glared angrily at Carter.

"What you want 'round here?"

She wore a dingy white cloth around her neck and a faded cotton wrapper belted too tightly about her lumpy figure. Her eyes snapped with curiosity from between folds of fat, and Carter knew he had better make some excuse.

"Excuse me, madam," he said, flipping his wallet open and shut in front of her face before she could blink. "Fire insurance inspection. This place is a menace."

"You're damned right it is. And for this the damned landlord charges us twice what the dump is worth!"

"Yes, madam, that is why I am here. To go after him."

"I hope you squeeze his balls!"

"Yes, madam."

He breathed a sigh of relief when she grunted an agreement, backed through the door, and slammed it behind her.

As he moved to the window he slipped Wilhelmina, a 9mm Luger, from a shoulder rig under his left armpit.

Through the stairs of the fire escape he could see the window. There was a flower-patterned curtain, but half of it had been drawn aside. He could just make out the corner of an old four-poster bed and a woman's bare foot.

He hesitated, weighing the idea of going across to the hall of the other building, when his mind was made up for him.

From beneath the sill, at the foot of the bed, the beefy face and bullet head of Emanuel, the bartender from the Casa del Mar nightclub, appeared. He had a glass of amber liquid in his hand and a leer a mile wide on his face.

If Carter could get out on the fire escape and climb a few steps above the window without being detected, he stood a pretty good chance of surprise.

He tried to open the window and found it stuck, painted shut.

"Goddamned place *is* a fire hazard," he hissed under his breath.

It took nearly five minutes' work with the point of the stiletto before the window groaned open. Gingerly he began to climb, keeping his eyes on the bartender's face for any sign that he was alerted.

Once he had enough height, he didn't hesitate. Moving his body around the side of the steps, he grasped a support bar and began to swing. He swung three times on the bar to make sure he had momentum, and then let go.

Just as he reached the glass, he kicked his legs out from the tuck and smashed through.

The room was lighted by a single dim ceiling bulb. Carter slithered across the floor amid a clatter of glass, and came to his feet in a half crouch as lightly as a cat.

In the single brief instant before the bedroom erupted into deadly violence, Carter saw the naked and twisted limbs of Lupe Vargas on the bed.

Her face and torso were obscured by the back and shoulders of a naked man on his knees beside the bed. Emanuel was still leaning over the foot of the bed, look-

ing down intently with sweat streaming from his face.
His eyes were filled with lascivious pleasure despite
smears of blood around his mouth.

Evidently Lupe Vargas had gotten in a few licks of
her own.

For one instant of paralyzed shock, the tableau held
its form. Then the kneeling man whirled with an inar-
ticulate oath, and Emanuel straightened up with a howl
of anger.

Carter coldly put a bullet in the center of Emanuel's
forehead before he was fully erect. The Killmaster
crouched on the floor not two feet from the naked
man's distorted face and slammed the solid weight of
the smoking Luger against the second man's jaw. It
made a solid chunk that shattered the jawbone, and his
feral eyes glazed as his body slumped limply to the floor
without a sound.

From the other building, through the shuttered bedroom window, Carter heard the wailing voice of the fat
woman in curlers. Evidently the shots, the sound of the
smashing window—or both—had brought her back out
of her apartment to investigate.

Hugo made short work of the ropes that tied the
woman to the bed. She ripped the gag from her own
mouth the second her hands were free.

"There's another one—somewhere in the front."

The Killmaster lurched toward the door and entered
the hall in a crouch. By now, number three had surely
realized something was very wrong.

He heard the scrape of a foot on the floor of the living
room, and went through the door in a roll.

The guy was big, about Emanuel's size, and waiting.
He landed a boot in the Killmaster's side and wrenched
Wilhelmina from his grasp. The Luger spun across the
floor and the man came at him like a bull.

Obviously he wasn't armed. And then Carter remembered a holster rig hanging on the bedpost. This one had probably already had his turn with Lupe Vargas.

Suddenly Carter felt a pair of huge hands around him, meeting at his spine. The man had tremendous strength, and Carter felt his body begin to bend back like a pretzel.

Carter's spine was on fire from whatever it might be that those educated fingers were doing to him back there. He spat full in the man's face, then blocked a knee as it hurtled up toward his crotch.

Carter didn't have any intention to fight it this way. He drew back an arm for as much distance as he could get, and then hammered a fist at the man's face. He was able to use his other hand, too, which surprised him a little when he realized that the guy was gripping his back tightly. As Carter aimed one punch after another at his face, the man's skin became puffy, the sections around his eyes darkening to a rust color, and the corners of his lips were wet with flecks of blood.

And while he punched the man, he had to stagger around the room with him. Carter never knew exactly when he realized that the man was trying to bend him backward, to crack his spine. His back felt as if a thousand porcupine quills had been jammed into it. No man's spine could take much more of this.

In spite of the pain, he realized that simply by forcing him back, the man was giving him a better target for a punch. But if Carter were going to take advantage of it, he knew he'd better be quick.

He aimed a fist full-strength against the Adam's apple bobbing before him.

Carter hadn't expected such a quick reaction. The man gurgled loudly, swaying as he tried to catch his breath and for the first time easing a little of the pressure on Carter. It happened with so much speed that Carter nearly missed his next chance to aim a harder punch at the same target.

He did it, though. The guy suddenly brought both hands around his throat and massaged it desperately. The look in his eyes now was murderous. Instead of wrestling again, he made a pair of fists and foolishly rushed Carter.

With savage pleasure, the Killmaster sidestepped the charge and hammerlocked the man's neck. One twist, with the aid of a knee in the small of the back, and it was all over.

He retrieved Wilhelmina and rushed back to the bedroom, only to come up short in the doorway.

Lupe Vargas had dressed, and now she was in the act of strangling the life from the naked man with one of the ropes from the bed.

"That's enough!" Carter barked.

"Is it?" she hissed through gritted teeth, her face flushed with the exertion of the kill.

"He's dead."

She turned it off like a faucet, dropped the lifeless body, and turned to Carter.

"I was set up by the girl at the club, and I think you've been had," he barked.

"I know I've been had."

"We can trade notes in the car. C'mon, let's get the hell out of here!"

Doors and windows were opening up and down the street, and faint cries of questions and alarm came through the twilight as Carter raced to the parked car, but no one got in his way.

He shoved the woman into the front seat and slid behind the wheel beside her, gunned the motor, and roared away to the first intersection without turning on the headlights. He made a screaming turn southward and continued two blocks without lights, slowed, then turned right decorously and switched on his lights.

Only then did he relax and let out a deep breath and take his eyes from the road ahead to look over at Lupe Vargas. She was staring back at him, her face like stone, calm, as if they were heading for a Sunday picnic.

"Evidently I opened a can of worms," he commented.

"Evidently we both did," she replied. "Reno has some kind of a business deal going with General Cordovan. Apparently it's been going on for years. My 'escape' from the country was engineered by Cordovan, and my meeting here with Reno was planned from the beginning."

"What do you think the business deal is?"

"Probably dope. All the money and information I sent to Esteban since I've been here was intercepted by Reno."

"With the help of little Amalia Persevez. She's the one who tried to set me up tonight. Were you able to get through?"

"Yes. I had a couple of contacts that Reno never knew about. Esteban was responsible for Ramón Baldez's kidnapping. He smuggled him into the country through Belize. But Esteban and his group never reached the main base camp."

"Where are they?"

"Who knows? Maybe hiding somewhere else in the mountains."

"Can you put me in touch with someone who can get me to Esteban?"

"Yes," she replied, calmly lighting a cigarette. "Me."

"You can't do that," Carter said, shaking his head.

"You're wanted in Guatemala. They'll shoot you on sight."

"This is a small island. If Reno finds me, *he'll* shoot me on sight."

"Touché," Carter growled. "Light me a cigarette."

"Do you have a way off Aruba?" she asked.

"Yeah. I've got a plane waiting at the airport."

She was silent for several moments, and then started laughing hysterically. "What an ass I've been. Reno knew who I was all the time and he was playing me along for Cordovan. And the worst part of it was . . ."

"Yeah?"

"I really enjoyed the runty little bastard in bed!"

She was silent the rest of the way to the airport.

Carter parked as close to the runway as possible, and then unlocked the trunk. When she saw the girl, Lupe calmly slapped her twice, hard. Amalia whined and tried to roll herself into a fetal position to avoid any more blows.

It did no good. Lupe Vargas dragged her from the trunk by the front of her blouse. It ripped in the process, exposing her heavy breasts.

"Tell Reno I'm gone, you hear?"

"Yes, yes!"

"And also tell him that if he ever leaves this island he'd better bring his army with him because I'm going to kill him. You hear?"

"Yes, I hear, I hear. Don't hurt me!"

"You aren't worth it," Lupe replied, and turned to Carter. "Let's go!"

Carter jogged to the plane with Lupe Vargas at his side. As he ran, he went over in his mind the best way of getting her past the immigration people in Belize.

EIGHT

Immigration proved to be no problem. One phone call to the British consulate brought a tall, sober-faced liaison man on the run.

Carter got him to the side and gave him a quick, mostly false story, but also informed the Britisher who he was and gave the man his security clearance.

"See here, it's highly irregular, you know. I don't think I can put the consulate in jeopardy . . ."

"Call Washington," Carter said curtly.

The man was back in fifteen minutes, explaining to the Belize immigration people that Mr. Carter's wife had lost her passport, but he would be glad to vouch for her as long as she was in the country.

"That won't be long," Carter said under his breath.

Twenty minutes later they were in the parking lot.

"Will there be anything else I can do?" the consular official said dryly, obviously just wanting to get rid of these two nuts.

Carter looked at Lupe Vargas. Her mouth silently formed the words "a car."

"We'll need a car."

"A car? At this hour? It's four o'clock in the morning! Impossible . . ."

"This your car?" Carter asked.

"Yes, but . . ."

"We'll drop you."

They did, and headed southwest out of the capital toward Benque Viejo and the frontier, with Lupe driving.

"We'll have to leave the car outside Benque Viejo and walk over the frontier. I know a place near the river where there are no patrols, but we must get over before dawn."

Carter settled back in the seat and let his eyes droop. It was obvious that Lupe Vargas knew exactly what she was doing.

He dozed, and only awakened when the car came to a halt.

"We walk now," she said, and before Carter could reply she was off.

Somehow she found a trail through the trees and thick underbrush. There was enough of a moon, even though it was partially blocked by the trees overhead, for Carter to follow her without breaking his neck.

Minutes later he could hear water rushing to their right. That would be the Belize River, and he knew they would follow it all the way into Guatemala.

"How long will it take?" Carter asked.

"With any luck, about another hour. There is a cave I know on the other side. We'll sleep there until the sun is up. By then the morning patrol boats will have passed and we can travel again. Do you have any money?"

"Yes, American."

"Good," she said with a chuckle. "That will buy anything."

She was like a mountain goat in the open and a snake in the underbrush, but Carter managed to stay with her.

Overhead, macaws and parrots screeched at the interlopers who passed, disturbing their sleep. The farther they went, the more Carter sensed the humid smell of decaying undergrowth.

Twice she came to a halt and crouched, listening intently to the night sounds of the jungle.

"Jaguar," she whispered. "Wait. He will pass."

Minutes later she would motion and they would move on.

Carter couldn't see the path that had been beaten through the undergrowth and the huge mahogany and ceiba trees, but she found it.

There was little doubt that Lupe had come this way many times before. She moved swiftly, with Carter directly behind her. Now and then there was enough light to see the lithe movement of her hips in the tight jeans she wore. He remembered how she had looked in the club standing beside the piano in that black dress in a pool of light.

For some odd reason she was even sexier now on her own turf.

"We are over the frontier," she said abruptly. "Now we climb."

And climb they did, for another half hour. Far below them Carter could see the river's black water gleaming through the underbrush. Somewhere in the distance he could hear the steady throb of a fishing boat's small diesel.

"Stay here!" she hissed, and was gone in the darkness.

Carter dropped to his haunches and listened intently to the insects for ten minutes until she returned.

"Come along and stay close. There is a ridge to our right . . . a very long fall to the river."

Carter did more than that. He curled a finger in one of her belt loops and became her shadow.

They waded across a rock-strewn mountain stream. On the other side was a strip of bare white rocks and an immense ceiba tree.

And then Carter saw it, the small mouth of a cave almost entirely hidden by the tree.

It was dark inside. Lupe knelt and a match flared. She made a small fire from dried moss. Quickly she added a few sticks and bits of bark lying on the cave floor, and then rose and went out. She was back almost immediately with an armload of wood.

"Isn't that a little dangerous? Won't someone see the light?" Carter commented.

"No," she replied, arranging the wood over the flames. "The entrance faces away from the river. If there are any army patrols, they will be on the river." Here she smiled. "The army is afraid of the jungle at night . . . for us it is home."

The ceiling of the cave was more than six feet high. Carter could stand erect comfortably. As the fire brightened, he could see that the cave went farther back, the walls curving outward and then going in again. There were a few boxes and a keg standing against one wall.

"What's that?" he asked.

"This was a stopover for refugees fleeing the government to Belize," Lupe replied. "It isn't used much anymore since that frontier is more heavily patrolled. Most of them go the other way now, to Mexico."

She moved over and pried open two of the boxes. From them she produced tinned beef and beans, some ragged blankets, and a Coleman lantern.

Together, silently, they prepared a meal and ate. Finished, they sat on the rough floor, warming themselves and watching the fire shadows dance on the walls of the cave. It was dark as velvet in the shadows outside the circle of light. A glimmer of gray marked the entrance.

Carter smoked, now and then darting his eyes to where Lupe sat, her arms around her knees, her head bent.

"Are you all right?"

"Yes. Sleep. It will be dawn in about an hour. We will leave when the fog lifts."

Carter suggested she would be more comfortable lying down, and if she wanted a pillow she could use his arm.

She didn't answer, nor did she move. He turned over and tried to sleep. But he could only doze. The body heat he had built up walking kept him warm for a time, until the predawn chill crept into his bones.

Lupe was still awake, sitting up with her head resting on her knees.

"Hey."

"What?"

"I'm frozen," Carter muttered. "Come and warm me."

She hesitated, then moved reluctantly across and he drew her down beside him. Wrapping his arms around her, he cuddled her round bottom into his stomach. It was like cuddling a life-size icicle.

"Something's wrong. What is it?"

"A feeling. I am part Indian, Maya. I get them."

"What feeling?"

"That Esteban Vargas is dead."

Dawn was peeking through the crack in the cave opening before Carter drifted off.

He awoke instantly with her hand on his shoulder. The fire had been rekindled and the cave was alive with the smell of cooking fish and coffee.

She was dressed in baggy white trousers, a matching peasant blouse, and a serape.

"I took some of your money and went to a nearby village. Your clothes are there. They will make us less conspicuous. Dress. Eat. We must go. I also bought two burros. They will let us travel faster."

Carter climbed into the new clothes and returned to the fire. In no time they devoured corn meal patties and several *robalos*, a tasty river fish.

Minutes later they were on their way. During the morning, the general direction they followed was southwest. The country they crossed now was partly wooded, particularly along the ravines, and it was soon evident that cover was more important to Lupe than time. Each time they would come to an open stretch, she would circle it, sometimes wasting an hour or more.

It was noon when they came upon a deserted village. It was not more than a half-dozen huts with thatched palm roofs and one long crumbling stone house.

"Where are we?"

"This is the village of San Pedro."

"It looks deserted."

"It is, except for the old man, Morales . . . the one we came to meet."

It was a ten-minute ride down the trail to the center of the village. During that time Lupe gave Carter a quick bio on Alberto Morales.

Years before, the government had stolen his land in the south. He had moved north. Again his land was taken, this time by the lumber companies. They did it by accusing him of harboring rebels. He was taken to Guatemala City where he was horribly tortured and put in prison.

That had been years before. When he was released at last, he armed himself and fled to the mountains where he joined the rebels for real.

But he didn't live with them. He fought his own war with the government, and often didn't agree with Esteban Vargas. Eventually both sides left him alone.

Now he lived like a hermit in the northern mountains,

but there was very little he did not know.

What was his connection to Lupe Vargas?

He was her uncle, her mother's brother, and he had taken Lupe in when her mother and father had disappeared.

In the center of the village, Lupe suddenly halted and slid off the burro.

Carter did the same, keeping his hand close to Wilhelmina where she rested in her shoulder rig beneath the serape.

"Morales?"

Silence.

She stepped away from the burro and shouted again. "Morales, it is Lupe!"

"I see you, little one. Who is the gringo?" The voice came from somewhere in the bowels of the stone house.

"The one who would talk with Esteban Vargas."

"Tell him to step away from the burro, and place the gun he carries beneath his serape on the ground."

"Do as he says."

"You're sure?" Carter said.

"I am sure, if you want his help. He also hates men from the north."

Carter reluctantly did as he was told. He had barely stepped back from the Luger when a man filled the doorless opening of the stone house.

He was short, but very broad and powerful, like a bear. His hair and eyebrows were pure white, and contrasted sharply with the tobacco-brown coloring of his face, which was lined and parched, scoured by wind and sun. His skin had actually been tanned into leather while he still lived.

His hands were full of M16, and there was a huge, old English Webley on his hip.

"The others?" Lupe asked.

"Gone. The army has been raiding heavily the past two days. They chased nearly everyone across the frontier into Mexico."

"Esteban as well?"

The old man shrugged. "We will eat and then talk."

Carter watched Morales move around the tiny kitchen preparing the food. He used his hands well, considering how they had been mutilated. After his torture, all he had left were knobby, rounded stubs for fingers. Both thumbs were intact, but all the fingers had been amputated at either the first or second joint, and now his hands looked more like thick, horny talons than anything human.

He carried two big steaming bowls of soup to the table and then made another trip for a block of cheese, a pan of tortillas and beans, and a jug of goat's milk.

He sat across from Carter and the woman, muttered grace in guttural Spanish, then took his knife and shaved thin flakes of cheese into his soup. The cheese formed a bubbly, viscous layer which he then sprinkled with beans. He then rolled a tortilla, dipped it into his soup and began eating.

After a moment he looked up at Carter. "Do my peasant table habits offend you?"

"No, not at all," Carter replied. "I was just marveling at how well you do everything with those hands."

Carter thought he detected a trace of a smile at the corners of the old man's mouth. Out of the corner of his eye he saw Lupe's eyes grow wide.

"Over the years I have learned to make do."

"Did the government of Baldez do that to you, or did it happen before Baldez?"

Morales shrugged. "All governments are the same . . . corrupt. Eat!"

Carter took two spoonfuls of the soup and a bite of tortilla and became ravenous. Between the three of them they ate everything and drank all the goat's milk.

When they were finished, Morales cleared the table and returned with a bottle of *caña*, the local firewater.

"Now we talk," he said, pouring. "What do you want?"

"What do you know of Esteban Vargas? Where is he?"

"I know that he took several men to the frontier a few nights ago. I know others of his group who waited for him and he didn't come. And then the soldiers came and drove them away."

"But not you?"

"The soldiers leave me alone because they cannot catch me. Also, I am mad. If they try to catch me, I will go to Guatemala City and kill all their leaders. They know I am not afraid to die. So they leave me alone."

"You sound as though you don't care what happens to Esteban Vargas."

"I don't," the old man said. "If Vargas got in power, he would be just like the others. Because he is a communist, your country would not want him to stay in power, so he would turn to the Russians. Eventually they would run the country."

Carter turned to Lupe. "Is this true?"

She shrugged. "That is why Esteban is no longer my man. I agree with my uncle."

"Then why did you keep helping him from Aruba?"

"I helped the wives and children of the men he led. It is they who suffer."

"Morales," Carter said, "will you get me to Vargas?"

The old man turned to Lupe. "What do *you* want, little one?"

She didn't hesitate. "Help him. The old Baldez is dying. The young Baldez is better than civil war."

The old man left, with a promise to be back by dusk. He said he would visit nearby villages. Someone would tell him the whereabouts of Esteban Vargas.

One of the huts was livable. Lupe made it ready for siesta while Carter fed the burros and gave them water.

It was midafternoon now. The insects and heat were more oppressive than ever. The heat was almost tangible, like something you could push and claw at.

When the burros were tethered in the shade, Carter headed for the hut. He noticed a large tank above it, and wondered idly if it were filled with water.

The answer came the moment he stepped inside. He could hear splashing and water running on the other side of a small partition.

"Lupe . . . ?"

"I'm here," came the reply.

Carter walked deliberately around the partition. It was a makeshift tin shower stall. He saw her just as she turned off the single valve, cutting off the water.

Long, clean legs, womanly hips, high proud breasts, jeweled with water. She had tied a towel around her long hair.

Carter heard the sudden thud of his own pulse in his ears. He didn't move, and she didn't try to cover her nakedness. Her eyes went cautious and then blank.

"Haven't you ever seen a naked woman before?"

"Hundreds of times, but not quite like you."

Silence, a full minute of it. He could see it in her face, in her proud breasts jutting, daring him. It was as if she were testing him.

"Hand me that towel," she said calmly.

He shook his head. "Get it yourself. I like to see you move around."

She shook her head impatiently and reached for the towel. He let her get her hand on it before he caught her wrist and pulled her roughly to him. For just a moment she fought against his solid strength, and then she stumbled against him and caught at his shoulder. His hands slid over her wet body.

"Why do you want me?"

"Because you're a woman."

For a brief second there was life in her eyes, then she dropped her head.

But her body quivered, came alive in his arms.

His blood pounded in him. His hands moved and he felt her slowly gathering more response. He heard a sudden, whispered exhalation of her breath in his ear and her weight clung more heavily against him.

They moved together through the doorway toward the bed. Her head was down, and he could not see the expression on her face. The room was dark and hot and filled with the small sounds they made.

He forced her head up, cupping his hand under her chin, and made her meet his eyes. In the gloom of the hug her dark eyes glittered with something he couldn't define. They were enormous, swimming darkly.

And suddenly they went blank again with that opacity he couldn't understand.

Her body was alive with wanting him. He could feel it.

But her mind was dead.

He dropped his hands. "I'll shower."

"Carter." Her voice stopped him at the partition. "Soon . . . perhaps."

He stripped and stepped under the tepid water.

NINE

They moved single file through the jungle for nearly two hours at a breakneck pace. Morales led, with Carter close behind him and Lupe Vargas bringing up the rear.

The old man had said little more than "Come" at the village as he shook them each awake.

Since then he had answered none of Carter's questions. Only grunted commands had come from him, and even they had ended nearly an hour before.

At last, in a clearing at the base of a small mountain, he halted. Without warning he ran his light around the trees and along the ground.

"It was here," Morales said. "There was a battle, much gunfire. There were helicopters and lights, powerful lights, that shined clear above the mountain."

"Who told you this, Morales?" Carter asked.

"Does it matter?"

"Maybe, maybe not. You yourself said there are both rebel and government spies and informers all through these mountains."

There was a growling chuckle from the old man's throat. "There are, but I know who they are, who to believe and who not to believe. I know the farmer and the hunter who goes his own way, who survives as I do and tells them all to go to hell. These men I believe. There was a fierce battle here a few nights ago."

Without another word he handed each of them a flashlight.

They didn't need to be told. Each of them fanned out.

It was Carter who found the first pile of spent cartridges. They were in two lines, now and then piles of high-caliber spent shells from a machine gun. Nearby he found the beaten-down grass and indentations where the helicopters had set down.

Lupe found patches of dried blood both on the ground and on the lower trunks of trees. Near each of these she found more spent shells, these from M16 rifles.

It was Morales who found the booted foot. It had been buried, but had been partially unearthed by an animal.

They dug with their bare hands and unearthed the body of a young boy dressed in green fatigues, a rifle, unfired, by his side.

Lupe knelt and gently brushed the dirt from his face in the illumination of Carter's flashlight.

"I know him," she said. "His name is Ricardo Montada. He is from the village of San Luis. He was only sixteen."

"There will be more," Carter growled.

"*Sí,*" Morales echoed, "it was an ambush. They didn't have a chance. I will get us something to dig with."

He moved into the darkness of the trees, and minutes later returned with three stout palm fronds. With his machete he chopped off the stem ends and then sheared them of needles. In no time he had shaved the ends to sharp edges so they became makeshift shovels.

Again they fanned out and began to dig.

They found the graves. Some of them with just a

single body, some with several, all had their arms buried with them. Some of them Lupe recognized; others were known to Morales.

It was near midnight when Morales called out to Carter. The Killmaster came across the clearing at a dead run just as the old man was hauling a corpse to the surface.

"Who is it?" Carter said, playing his light over the body.

"Vargas," Morales intoned.

The rebel leader's torso was riddled with bullet holes from a machine gun. His uniform had been almost shredded by the fusillade. Carter let out his breath in a long sigh. His face was like stone as he stepped forward and stared at the bloody remains. He tasted bile in his throat. He suddenly felt cold.

A quick, shuddering gasp came from behind them and he looked up and saw Lupe with both hands pressed hard across her mouth.

"Get away," he said harshly.

"Oh, my God . . ."

"I told you to get away." Carter straightened and pushed her back toward the clearing.

"Bastards!" she cried.

Suddenly her solid composure cracked and she was in his arms, weeping. Carter held and rocked her until it subsided.

"There is a village nearby with a priest. I will get men . . ."

"No," Carter said.

"What?"

"No. I want whoever did this to be in the dark that we know. We can't risk that someone in the village will talk."

"But why?" Morales roared.

"Because, if they are tipped, Ramón Baldez will be dead ten minutes later."

Lupe stepped away from him. "I know who did this, and so do you. And you know who has the young Baldez."

Carter nodded. "Now that I have proof, yes, I think I know. But before we do anything, I must get Baldez back. Now let's bury them all again."

But before they started, Carter took photographs, a lot of photographs, with a special high-speed night camera, and close-ups of faces and wounds with the aid of the high-powered flashlights.

It took nearly two hours to rebury the bodies and then shovel leaves and vegetation back over the graves.

"Believe me," Carter said when they were finished, "the world will know just as soon as I have rescued Baldez."

It was after midnight when they got back to the village.

"There is someone in the Yucatán who works with me," Carter told Lupe Vargas. "You can go there with me in the morning. It is a safe house. You'll be all right there until this is over. Then, don't worry, I'll make sure you can come back to your country with a full pardon."

He left her and Morales together in the stone house, and stumbled to the hut.

He stripped and lay down on the bed in nothing but his shorts. He lay there, dog tired, almost naked, feeling his muscles relax, willing his body to lose its tenseness. He tried to think beyond the morning, but his thoughts were hazy, unclear.

He willed his mind to sleep, but he could only become drowsy.

It was about a half hour later when he sensed her

enter the hut. She crossed to her own cot and he heard her undress. There was a thin shaft of moonlight across the cot. He saw her drop into it and settle, her back to him.

Carter squinted. She was curled up on the narrow bed, on her side, her legs pulled up, her hip a lovely curve in the darkness.

"Nick . . ."

It was the only time she had ever called him by his first name. "Yes?"

"I'm afraid. For the very first time in my whole life, I am afraid."

"It will all finish right. I'll see to it. Go to sleep."

"I wasn't crying, back there, just for Esteban. I was crying for all of them."

"I know."

"Do you?"

"Believe me, I do."

There was a long silence, and then she rolled over, exposing all of her moonlit shimmering beauty to his eyes.

"Do I have to come over there?"

He hesitated. "You're sure?"

"I've never been more sure," she whispered, her voice suddenly very husky.

He stepped across the narrow space, dropping his shorts in the process. He lay down beside her, facing her. She slithered closer until her breath was warm on his cheek.

"Why?" he said, not really knowing why he asked.

"If it matters, I'll tell you."

"It matters."

"Because now I think you really care what happens to all of us."

She slid one arm under his body and the other across his waist, and her head rested in the curve of his arm.

She wiggled, fitting her body into all the curves of his body and then raised her head to kiss his neck, his chin, and then his lips. She sighed heavily and her breathing quickened, her breasts rising against him in a way that sent the flow of juices racing through him, stepping up the beat of his heart, bringing a strong fluid feeling, making him immensely tall and powerful and heavy with want.

He rolled her on her back gently, revealing a lovely breast. He caressed a nipple between thumb and forefinger, and then bent to place it between his lips, tickling it with his tongue, pressing down with his teeth. He moved his mouth to her shoulder, bit down, her fingers alternately digging and caressing. Her head was thrown back, her back arched, her hips flowing forward to meet him.

Suddenly she was like a writhing animal beneath him, and Carter knew this was the woman he sensed in Aruba.

"Yes . . . yes . . . slowly."

Her murmuring sigh filled his ears as his hands moved over her body. She clasped them, forcing them tighter against her, her eyes closing as she lay there in silence, waiting for him. Lightly, his fingertips ran down her thigh. She breathed heavily and turned her head, greedily fastening her mouth on his parted lips. Something of her awakening wildness was transmitted to him.

He took her chin in his hand and kissed her lips, her eyes, and then her lips again before he ran his tongue lightly down her neck and enfolded the heavy warmth of her breast in the fullness of his hand. He fondled the globe of loveliness, stirring her deeply, until she turned feverishly, gathering frenzy like a hurricane, pressing against him with a vast shuddering sigh, crushing him in her arms and kissing him with an open, savage hunger.

They were locked in a tight, coordinated precision and her body moved to meet his with nerve-exposed awareness, with a black-velvet smoothness.

He felt her soft hands guiding him into her, then releasing him to grip him to her while moving her body, dragging him deeper and deeper.

They moved joyously together, reveling in the physical nearness, her hands searching, their mouths locked together, their bodies fused in a union of passion that consumed without destroying.

Then he floated downward slowly, down to a place where he was aware of the quivering, gradually diminishing spasms of her ripe body, and he whispered in her ear, her arms tightening around him, letting him know that she felt as he did, full and satiated.

It was the rain that brought him awake. It was a steady, driving downpour that made odd, almost caressing, sounds on the thatch of the roof.

He sat up, rubbed his eyes, and glanced over at the other cot. She was already up and out. Pulling on his pants, he walked to the doorless opening.

It was a tropical rain, coming down in sheets so thick Carter could hardly see beyond twenty feet. It would be a bitch traveling, he thought, but travel he must. His seventy-two hours were almost up.

Through the rain he could make out the smoke of a cookfire curling up from the stone house chimney. Automatically, his stomach growled.

He finished dressing and lurched through the rain at a jog. He was two steps inside the stone house when he sensed something was not right.

The old man, Morales, sat at the rough log table, a pipe clenched between his teeth, his hands deftly reassembling the recently cleaned and oiled M16.

Carter's eyes took in the rest of the dim interior in one glance.

No Lupe Vargas.

"Where is she?"

"Gone," the old man replied, barely glancing up from the table, "before dawn."

"Where?"

He shrugged. "She didn't say, but she said she would be back."

"When?"

"Probably long after you are gone."

"But why?"

Here Morales paused, taking the pipe from his mouth. "This team you say you will put together. They are good?"

Carter hadn't read the contents of the envelope in the Yucatán, but he had faith in David Hawk. "The best, all specialists."

"That is good, but you will waste precious time trying to find out where they are holding Ramón Baldez. Between Lupe and myself we will have that information for you when you return. Sensible, no?"

"Sensible, yes, if she doesn't get herself killed or arrested."

Morales smiled the first smile Carter had seen since he met him. "Lupe can take care of herself."

Carter remembered the scene he had witnessed in Aruba when he had walked in and found her strangling her tormentor.

"Yeah," the Killmaster said dryly, "I suppose she can."

A slicker sailed across the room. Carter caught it.

"Eat. I will guide you to the frontier."

Carter wolfed down tortillas and beans, and a half

hour later they were making their way down the mountain.

In less than a mile they were both soaking wet even with the shoulder-to-ankle slickers. But Carter quickly realized that the rain was their ally. It hid them from view and allowed them to travel nearly twice as fast as he and Lupe had done coming in.

It was nearly noon when Morales called a halt. He motioned Carter to join him and they hunkered down beside a tree.

"What's wrong?"

"We wait," the old man said, taking out his pipe. "The frontier is right down there."

Carter didn't ask why he couldn't just go on across. By now he knew that Morales had a very good reason for everything he did, and he would tell Carter about it when he got good and ready.

When the pipe was going good, he spoke again. "Do you know Guatemala City?"

Carter nodded. "Fairly well."

"How soon will you return?"

"Two, perhaps three days. We'll probably come in from different directions."

"Good. You, yourself, must stay at the Hotel Camino Real."

Carter closed his eyes in concentration. "Hotel Camino Real. Reforma, at Fourteenth Street."

"Very good. Be in your room at three and six each day. If you are not contacted at these times in two days, go to the Blisters cantina at eight o'clock the evening of the second day. You will be contacted there."

"The Blisters cantina."

"Yes . . . shhh . . ."

Carter hardly took a breath. Then he heard it, the

sound of a small plane coming nearer and nearer. Seconds later it was directly overhead, and soon after that passing on. Some minutes later the sound of its engine died away completely.

"Border patrol," Morales said, "spotter plane. Makes a pass up the border every day at noon. It is safe to cross now. Your memory is good?"

"Yes," Carter said, rising with the other man.

"Then I will see you in Guatemala. *Hasta la vista, gringo*."

He turned away, and seconds later disappeared in the driving rain and the jungle.

Maybe, Carter thought, turning toward the frontier, getting Ramón Baldez back would be easier than it appeared on the surface.

TEN

The airport was the same, the open jeep with the roll bar was the same, and so was the elfin face with pursed lips staring up at him.

Carter put everything he could into the kiss, but it made no dent.

"She must have been something," Estrella Gomez said, dropping back to her heels and stepping away.

"Who?"

"Whoever she was down south."

Carter smiled and curled his fingers in the thick hair at the nape of her neck as they careened out of the parking lot. "She was."

It was enough. When you're in the business long enough, you learn: today is today and there may be no tomorrow.

"What's new?" Carter asked as they hit the mountain and the jeep found the gate through the adobe fence.

"I've got the scrambler line set up. They want you to report in the minute you arrive."

Estrella slid the jeep to a halt and they both entered the house. Carter helped himself to a beer while she unlocked the safe and set up the phone. When it was ready he handed her the two rolls of special film he had snapped at the Guatemala grave site.

"Can you do these up fast?"

"Sure," she said, nodding. "Two hours, give or take."

"Great. Make eight-by-tens, a pair for each negative."

"Will do."

She disappeared, and Carter sat at the desk. He took a few seconds to formulate his thoughts, took a deep breath, and dialed.

It was picked up on the second ring, and the instant Carter heard Ginger Bateman's voice he also heard the scrambler kick in.

"Is the man there?"

"Yeah, and chomping at the bit. You used most of your seventy-two hours."

"It was productive. Put him on."

He heard Ginger on the office intercom and the clicks as the recorders were turned on, and then the cigar-gruff voice of David Hawk.

"Talk to me, N3."

Carter talked. He retold the events in Aruba concerning Lupe Vargas that eventually led them to Guatemala and the mass graves.

"You're sure it was Esteban Vargas?" Hawk asked.

"Positive. All three of us identified him, and I've got pictures . . . detailed pictures. Gomez is developing them now. We should have a set on your desk by this evening."

There was a long pause on the other end of the line. Carter could almost hear the gears in the other man's mind grinding away.

"Do you think you can trust these two?" Hawk asked at last.

"As much as anyone down there can be trusted. Also, Lupe agrees with Interpol. The assassinations were the work of Venezzio."

"But we don't have time now to chase him all over the world."

"Right," Carter growled. "If I can get Ramón Baldez out to safety, there's a pretty good chance we can get enough on Cordovan to hang him without collaboration from Venezzio. As far as I'm concerned, everything points to Cordovan setting himself up to take over."

Hawk chuckled. "Not much doubt of that, but proving it may take more than we're capable of right now."

"Lupe Vargas seems to think the general is thick with a hood on Aruba named Reno Poppi. Can you check that out? It might be another nail in Cordovan's coffin if we can tie them together."

"Bateman," Hawk barked, "are you on?"

"Yes, sir."

"Get on this Poppi."

"Will do, sir."

There was a click as Ginger Bateman left the line.

In short, terse sentences, Hawk brought his number one agent up to date on recent developments in Guatemala.

"Cordovan claims that he has routed nearly all the rebels, but his army has not been able to find Ramón Baldez. He held a press conference this morning and said that he is agreeing to the ransom."

Carter groaned. "And right after it's paid, Ramón Baldez's body will appear. Cordovan is ten million richer, and Vargas and his rebels are blamed for the death."

"That would be a reasonable scenario, I think. You'll have to go in, and fast, N3."

For the next half hour, the two men bounced a plan back and forth between them. With the additional help of Lupe Vargas and Morales, the situation was simplified.

Finally Carter hung up. He got a fresh beer and then retrieved the thick manila folder from the safe. He cracked the seal, withdrew the material, and read it through completely. Then he read it again, synthesizing its contents in his mind.

Jeeter Ferris: Nam vet, weapons expert, and hand-to-hand combat genius. Became a mercenary in South America after leaving the military. Got caught on the losing side and did five years in prison. Retired and married, now running a sport fishing shop in Puerto Vallarta, Mexico.

Smiley Lassiter: Ex-RAF pilot. Absolutely fearless. Can fly anything from a 747 to a helicopter. Runs a small charter service in the Caribbean based on St. Thomas. Known to be having financial problems.

Jake Tory: Ex-Marine drill sergeant. Became an expert on guerrilla fighting and lost his citizenship for teaching the wrong people. Currently a bodyguard for a rich German planter in Rio. Rumored to be drinking heavily.

Mohammed Namali: Expert explosives man. Learned his trade with terrorist groups, but eventually rebelled and turned several of them in. Got a raw deal in France, so decided to turn his talents to safecracking. He is now wanted on twenty-three warrants by French authorities. Believed to be hiding somewhere in Tangier.

Carter smiled to himself. Good men all. They were wild, but Carter knew each of them, and was sure that under the right conditions he could control them.

Also, they fit Hawk's requirements as set down in a handwritten note:

N3: All of these men are known outlaws as far as our government is concerned. Should an unfortunate occurrence befall the operation and one or more of them fall into the wrong hands, none of them could be connected to any of our agencies. Good luck.

The last dossier was on his contact inside the country. Her name was Dominique Navarro. She was the daughter of an old aristocratic Guatemalan family. Early on she hooked up with the Baldez regime, and because of her American education and her high-level contacts in Washington, Baldez used her often as a diplomat without portfolio. She also had the old man's complete confidence on matters of intelligence inside and outside the country.

With Lupe Vargas on the scene, Carter thought, there might not even be a need to contact Dominique Navarro.

He memorized all the salient facts and burned the dossiers. He kept the current photographs of each of them, and the false passport and other identifying papers that would get him into the country as Jules Blackmer, a tin dealer.

This done, he stripped and showered but didn't shave. He only trimmed his beard and hair enough so he could pass through airports without arousing suspicion as an unkempt mad bomber.

In a closet he found an array of clothes in six different sizes. He chose a light blue shirt, dark slacks, and a safari jacket. He had just finished packing an additional change and some toilet articles, when Estrella entered the room.

Wordlessly she spread the dry prints out on the bed. "Pretty grim."

"Yeah, these boys don't fool around. They're after big stakes. Get a set off to Washington. Keep a set here in the safe, just in case."

She nodded. "I'm to help you any way I can."

"You can help a lot," Carter said, putting the tools of his trade in the special lead-lined bottom of a bag. "I want you to go to Tangier, posthaste."

"And . . . ?"

"Find this guy." He handed her the photo of Mohammed Namali. "It won't be easy. He's wanted, and pretty touchy."

"And when I find him?"

"Do nothing. Just spot him. Check into the Hotel Les Almohades. I'll call every day. As soon as I've contacted the others, I'll join you."

Carter was heading out the door, bag in hand. When the scrambler phone rang, Estrella grabbed it.

"It's Bateman . . . for you."

"Yeah?"

"I ran down your Reno Poppi."

"And?"

"And Mr. Poppi, his driver, and a woman named Amalia Persevez were separated from the living this morning at nine o'clock by a car bomb."

"Shit," Carter hissed.

"Want me to stay on it?"

"Yeah. Dig. Maybe we can still make a connection between Poppi and Cordovan."

"Will do. And you?"

"I'm heading for Mexico, Puerto Vallarta."

"The game begins," she said dryly.

"That it does."

Estrella Gomez locked everything up behind her and joined him in the jeep. All she carried was a large burlap shoulder bag.

"Is that it?" Carter asked, indicating the bag.

"That's it . . . a change of underwear, passport, and money. Travel light. It's the nature of the business."

"How well I know," Carter said, and settled down in the seat to let his mind refine his moves in the days ahead.

ELEVEN

Carter followed the directions off the main road, then off the secondary road onto two well-worn ruts that led to the place the locals called El Jeeters. It was down the coast about fifteen miles south of Puerto Vallarta in what could only be termed the low rent district.

He crossed over a bridge that barely held the rental compact's weight, and took the lefthand pair of ruts at a fork. He could smell the ocean again now and knew he was heading directly for it.

Then he burst through the trees to the beach. There were four buildings, three small ones huddled darkly together at the edge of the inlet of his left, and a larger one just ahead and to his right. Bright light and heat vapors emanated from the open door of the larger building. Beyond it Carter could see a worse-for-wear pier jutting out into the ocean.

The only car was an ancient station wagon that looked like the recent victim of a demolition derby.

Carter cut his lights and got out.

"Who is it?" a woman's voice called in terrible Spanish from outside the doorway. She was standing to one side of it away from the light.

"Name's Carter," he answered in English. "I just drove down from Puerto Vallarta. Jeeter around?"

"Took a party out about a half hour ago . . . won't be back until around midnight."

Carter was almost to the door when she stepped out. She was a thin blonde with long curly hair and good legs. She was wearing cut-offs and a halter top that showed off breasts much too large for the rest of her.

She was also cradling a sawed-off Remington in the crook of her right arm.

"Lot of punks come down here at night to raise hell. Like I said, Jeeter won't be back until midnight."

"I'll wait, if you don't mind. Got a beer?"

"Yeah, come on in."

He followed her in. The illumination inside the crudely finished room came from a hissing gasoline lantern suspended from a rafter with a length of wire. Insects whirled about it in a frenzied dance, butting their heads against the shield. On the left was a short counter with three stools before it, and beyond the end of the counter was a glass-topped showcase containing items of fishing tackle. There was a small screened window at the other end of the room, and an open doorway at the left behind the pass-through between the ends of the counter and the showcase. This presumably led to their living quarters in the rear of the building. Behind the counter was a small refrigerator and a bottled-gas stove that had two burners and a grill. On the shelves above the stove were some cartons of cigarettes, cans of soup and condensed milk.

All in all, it wasn't hard for Carter to figure out that Jeeter Ferris wasn't setting the world on fire financially.

He climbed one of the stools while she set the shotgun down, stuck an already lit butt in the corner of her mouth, and produced a Dos Equis.

"That's fifty pesos Mexican, two bucks if you got American."

Carter laid a twenty on the counter.

"I ain't got no change."

"That's all right. Have one yourself."

"Hot damn, a big spender."

She popped the cap on a second Dos Equis and drained half of it in one long swallow. Up close she looked all of her years and even rougher than she sounded.

"What do you want with my old man?"

"You must be Mrs. Ferris."

"Florence. What do you want with Jeeter?"

"Business." Carter sipped his beer. It was warm.

Her eyes narrowed. "What kind of business?" Suddenly she leaned forward. "I think I know your type. My Jeeter ain't goin' junglin' no more, you hear? He can't make no livin' in some spic jailhouse."

"You know that, Flo . . . can I call you Flo?"

"I think you're a smartass."

"You know, I haven't eaten anything since this morning. I sure could use an old-fashioned American hamburger if you've got a patty back there."

"You are a smartass."

"And another beer. And have another yourself, Flo."

She was fuming, but she produced another beer and then stormed to the refrigerator. When the light was lit under the grill, she slapped down the meat patty and fired up another cigarette in the corner of her mouth.

"If Jeeter goes off junglin' again, I'll divorce the bastard."

"Believe me, Flo, I wouldn't break up a happy home."

He watched her fume for another minute and then turned away. A bug banged into the lantern overhead and fell to the counter where it lay on its back, buzzing its wings. The meat began to sizzle after a minute or two and she turned it with the spatula, leaning forward with the mane of hair swinging downward across her cheek. A roach came up from somewhere and walked along the edge of the counter. It looked shiny in the white, hot light. She stared at it, and then pushed the hair back from her face with her hand.

"Grease," she said, almost in a whisper.

His eyes turned, but he made no other movement. "What?"

"I said grease. G-r-e-a-s-e."

"What about it?"

"Nothing. I love the smell of it in my hair."

"You sure as hell have a hard time," he said.

"What gave you that idea?" she asked. "Not many women can go around smelling like they slept with their head on a rancid tortilla."

Something made her look up then, and she caught his eyes on her. She stopped abruptly. The room was caught up in that taut silence again.

"God, I hate Mexico."

"It can be a hard life down here," Carter said, "when you have to scratch for every dollar."

"Yeah." Again her eyes narrowed. "Maybe it wouldn't be so bad if Jeeter went off junglin' after all."

From there it was a silent truce until midnight.

They heard the boat dock and a growling voice direct the two fishermen to their rooms. A moment later Jeeter Ferris stepped into the room.

He hadn't changed an iota in the five years since Carter had last seen him. He was over six feet, but rail thin, with a bleak and angular face that seemed to have been stretched too tightly over the bone structure behind it.

Jeeter Ferris was how he looked, as functional and

uncluttered as the sharp blade of an ax.

His gray eyes were dull and blank until they fell on Carter.

"Well, kiss my Oakie butt, where the hell did y'all come from!"

Carter smiled. "According to your wife, from under a rock. How's tricks, Jeeter?"

"Same as always, broke on my ass. I just can't seem to turn a dollar when it's an honest one. But then you got eyes, Nick."

"Can we talk?"

"Sure. Flo . . ."

"Yeah?"

"Those two idiots want some beer in their cabin."

She rambled around for a full two minutes, then stormed out.

"Nice lady," Carter said.

"Don't pound sand up my ass. She's a mean-tempered scarecrow with tits. Now, what's up?"

"A job, in Guatmo, springing a VIP. You still got contacts?"

Ferris nodded. "Anything up to a tank."

"What's your boat?"

"Aquilar, fifty-footer. Two Chrysler marines side by side. They'll deliver six hundred horses. She'll do sixty-five on flat water and outrun anything south of San Diego."

Carter smiled. "So fishing isn't your only business."

Ferris smiled. "Was it ever? But business has been bad. What you payin', Nick?"

"Twenty-five big ones, plus expenses and your passport back if we pull it off."

"My, my. What's the chances of comin' out alive?"

"On a scale of one to ten, I'd say about a five."

"Hot damn, sounds like good odds to me!"

"Then you're in?"

"Up to my ass, Nicky, up to my ass."

It took an hour to feed Jeeter Ferris all his instructions, and then Carter headed back to Puerto Vallarta. There he grabbed four hours' sleep in a hotel and caught the early-morning flight to Mexico City with a connection to Rio.

Jake Tory was tall, with a barrel chest and the shoulders of a weight lifter. But right now those shoulders were sagging as he stepped from the car and gently shut the door behind him.

Far below, the lights of Rio twinkled. To his left the big plantation house was dark. To his right, moonlight bathed the pool house.

His employer, old Hans Kohner, would be sleeping peacefully in the big house. His wife, Monta, would be waiting in the pool house for Jake.

The call had come an hour earlier. Jake had known it would come eventually. He'd known since the first moment he met the woman a couple of days after Hans had hired him six months ago.

It had been in her eyes when she looked at Jake: *You may guard my husband's body, but you'll service mine!*

She was the first woman Jake had ever met who made his skin crawl.

"Jake, this is Monta Kohner," the voice on the phone had purred.

"Yes, Mrs. Kohner?"

"Oh, Jake, after six months I think you can call me Monta."

"What can I do for you . . . Mrs. Kohner?"

"A lot, Jake . . . you can do a lot for me," she had said, sighing heavily into the phone. "I'm going to take a swim, Jake, and then I'll be in the pool house."

"Look, Mrs. Kohner . . ."

"It's Monta, Jake . . . the pool house, one hour."

He had thrown the phone across the room, cursed, had four quick drinks, and then cursed some more.

But he had gotten in his car and driven up the mountain. And now he was heading toward the pool house like the servant she had told him he was.

Jake had a sweet deal with Hans Kohner and he didn't want to lose it.

"But, shit," he growled out loud, "this is too damned much!"

The upward path was narrow and winding through the trees, and the short grass underfoot deadened the sound of his steps. He continued to move doggedly forward and eventually came out by the pool.

He listened intently before stepping into the moonlight. The cottage stood dark and silent in front of him. Over his left shoulder he could see the dark hulk of the Kohner mansion without a light showing. As far as any outward signs went, he was the only person awake on the mountain.

But he knew differently.

He closed his eyes for a few seconds, blanked his mind, and stepped out into the moonlight toward the silent cottage.

The door opened easily under his hand. He stepped in and closed it behind him.

He held his breath for a long moment and listened, closing his eyes to adjust them more quickly to the dark. Blood drummed loudly in his ears and he could hear no other sound. But there was an intangible *feel* of some other living being close to him. An odor, perhaps, or an otherworldly emanation that touched off his battle-honed senses.

He opened his eyes and said quietly, "Where are you?"

Then he saw her. The shimmering whiteness of flesh standing not more than ten feet from him. The figure did not move and it didn't speak.

He moved toward her.

She waited for him to come. Without moving and without speaking. When he had covered half the distance he was conscious of the smell of her body. The thing he had sensed on first entering without being quite aware what it was.

The figure became less ghostlike and more real. There were two white limbs and a white torso and white arms outstretched to enfold him in her embrace. It was just like the bitch to put on a show like this, he thought with irrational anger as he neared her. She must have read in some book that women should be mysterious and silently alluring.

"All right, dammit," he hissed, "I'm here."

"I know," she said, and sighed. "God, but you are big."

She surged forward against him and her hot arms were around his neck before he could avoid the embrace. She pressed her body against him and pressed her mouth on his, clinging fiercely about his neck with surprising strength. His hands went behind her back instinctively, and he found it sinewy and strong, the flesh firm and fever-hot beneath his hands.

It all happened in seconds, and it was seconds more before Jake's dazed comprehension told him the facts. This was a mature and lustful woman, crazed with desire and with waiting in the night for a man to come to her. She was moaning queerly now, speaking broken phrases, struggling with all her strength to pull him off his feet so they would go to the floor together.

From an angry determination to fight off her advances, Jake's mood swiftly changed to one of answering passion. He had no time to question. He was confronted in the darkness with a woman whose ardor aroused his own, and his arms tightened about her and he staggered forward two steps to the dim outline of a couch against the wall.

As they fell, her fingers entwined savagely in his hair.

When at last she sank back, limp and exhausted, Jake lifted himself on both elbows to stare down at the white oval of her face beneath his.

Her eyes were closed and her lips parted to let little breaths in and out.

"That was very good, Jake. Much better than I expected."

Jake Tory closed his eyes and counted to ten slowly. When he finished, he rolled to his side and fumbled in his jacket for a cigarette.

He snapped his lighter and put flame to the cigarette. She opened her eyes to smile dreamily up at him. She was almost beautiful in her blissful state of contentment. Her features were softened, her eyes moist and bright, her nostrils wide at the base and quivering under his gaze.

"Could I have a cigarette, please?" she asked huskily.

Jake got out a cigarette and inserted it between her parted lips. Her eyelids came down as he thumbed his lighter again. She drew smoke deep into her lungs and murmured, "Thanks."

"For the cigarette?"

"For everything. You're . . . what I knew you'd be."

"You're not," he told her bluntly.

The burning tip of her cigarette flared as she sucked

in smoke again. Her lips were smiling.

"You'll have to give me a key to your apartment, of course."

"I will?"

"Of course. It really isn't safe up here, you know."

"Look, Mrs. Kohner . . ."

"Monta."

"Okay, Monta. This is a one-time shot . . . *fini*, get it?"

She yawned and stretched sensuously. "No, I don't get it, Jake. This is the first of *many* times."

Inside he was boiling, and he could feel a flush of rage rising in his face. "What about your husband?"

"What about the old fool?"

"That 'old fool' pays me a lot of money."

"I know, Jake, darling," she said, stretching voluptuously again, "and he'll keep paying you a lot of money as long as you're a good boy."

Jake could feel his fuse burning low. She stubbed her cigarette out against the wall beside her and reached for him with avid fingers.

"But let's not waste time talking about my husband," she purred.

"I spent twelve years in the Marine Corps."

"What does that have to do with anything?"

"I was the most decorated man in my outfit . . ."

"Kiss me, Jake." But he was already on his feet and pulling on his clothes. "What the hell do you think you're doing?"

"Kissing you off, honey."

"Like hell you are. You walk out that—"

The flat of his hand against her cheek was like the crack of a rifle in the small cottage. The next thing Monta Kohner knew she was across his broad shoulders like a sack of potatoes and he was heading out the door.

"Put me down!" she screamed. "Damn you, put me down!"

He did, right in the middle of the swimming pool without breaking stride.

He reached the car, with her screaming still in his ears. So absorbed was he that he had the car started and backed around before he sensed the figure in the back seat.

"That's no way to treat a lady, Jake."

His reflexes were like lightning. The Colt was out of his shoulder holster and he was whirling in the same movement.

"What . . . Carter, I'll be damned!"

"You're losing your touch, Jake. I trailed you all the way up here and you didn't even spot me."

"I had a lot on my mind."

Carter crawled over the seat and lit a cigarette. "The lady?"

"That bitch is no lady!"

Carter chuckled. "Did she spurn your advances?"

Jake roared with laughter. "Would you believe it was the other way around? Well, what the hell, I was looking for a job when I found this one."

The back wheels sprayed gravel as Jake dropped it into gear and they headed down the mountain.

"Does that mean you're unemployed, Jake?"

"Yeah. Whatcha got in mind."

"A job."

"I'm in."

"Don't you want to know what it's all about?"

"Hell, no," Jake said, laughing all the louder. "You can tell me who I gotta kill later."

"Drop me at the airport," Carter replied. "I'll fill you in on time and places on the way."

TWELVE

It was five o'clock in the afternoon by the time Carter arrived at Truman Airport on the island of St. Thomas. As soon as he was through customs he hit a phone booth.

After many frustrating false starts, he finally got through to the Les Almohades in Tangier. He sighed with relief when the telephone in Estrella Gomez's room was picked up.

"It's me. What have you got?"

"Sore feet so far, and a dwindling change purse. Your bird Namali is a very hard man to pin down. He most certainly doesn't want to be found."

"Have you got anything?"

"A couple of leads, but they're tricky. It seems it isn't only the French police who would like to get their hands on our boy."

"Well, stay on it. I'm in St. Thomas. I'll be staying at the Pavilions. Leave a message at the desk if I'm not in."

"Will do. How goes your end?"

"Two in. I'm heading for Lassiter's now."

"I'll stay in touch."

Carter hung up. He hired a car and got a pinpoint on Smiley Lassiter's address from the girl at the desk.

It was a ten-minute drive from the airport and another fifteen minutes to locate the address. It was in one of the new condominiums that seemed to have sprung up everywhere recently.

There was an air of ritzy splendor about the setup that brought a smile to Carter's lips. It was just like Smiley to live in such pseudo-opulence. The dossier had said that the ex-RAF pilot was in financial trouble; he wondered if Washington had their information right.

He climbed a long flight of stairs to the second floor and walked along miles of terazzo-paved galleries, glad of the cool Caribbean breeze as he trudged along checking each door number.

He finally arrived at a heavy studded oak door marked 177-L, and stopped in front of it with a sigh of relief. He put his finger on the bell and didn't bother to take it off.

Carter began to think Lassiter wasn't at home after a full sixty seconds had passed without any response to his ringing. He frowned but kept his finger on the button.

After one minute and forty seconds of steady ringing, his stubbornness brought results. The knob turned and the heavy door swung inward soundlessly.

In a small foyer lighted from floor lamps in the long living room beyond an archway, a girl confronted him. She was barefooted and wore a short mandarin robe. Her hair was cut as short as a boy's, and she was rubbing her eyes sleepily with both fists and yawning widely. She didn't actually look at Carter as she spoke.

"So they let you out, you jerk. Why didn't you use your key?"

Carter stepped inside, closed the door, and took her firmly by the elbow.

She dropped her knuckles from her eyes and blinked up at him in round-faced amazement.

"Who are you? Oh, Christ, you're not from the landlord . . ."

"No. The name is Carter. Who are you?"

"Barbara from Cardiff and I wish I were back there right now."

She turned away from him into a large inner room that had a ceiling two stories high and a railed balcony on three sides at the second-floor level.

"Smiley wouldn't be around, would he?"

"He hasn't been around for two days," she said, curling up on a sofa and tucking her bare legs under her. "You wouldn't have anything to drink on you, would you?"

"I'm afraid not. Is Smiley on a run?"

"No."

"Well, when do you expect him back?"

"I don't know."

"You know something, Barbara-from-Cardiff?"

"What?"

"It's a bitch getting any information out of you."

"What do you want to know?"

"Where's Smiley?"

"In jail."

"Oh, shit," Carter groaned, flopping into a chair opposite her and lighting a cigarette.

"Can I have one of those?"

He passed her the lit one and fired another. "What happened?"

"It was three days ago . . . nights, really. The bank wouldn't extend his loan on the planes, so he was depressed. You a friend of Smiley's?"

"Yeah. Go on."

"If you're a friend of Smiley's, then you know he likes to spend money when he's depressed. He also likes to drink. He took me out to one of those fancy restaurants on Fortuna Bay to celebrate his impending bankruptcy."

"If he's so broke, how does he afford all this?" Carter asked, swinging his arm in an arc around the room.

"He doesn't. The rent's four months past due."

"I see. Go on."

"Well, we went into the bar to have *a* drink before dinner. Only we never got around to dinner. Smiley just kept drinking and bitching about all the rich, lard-butted tourists with cameras growing out of their noses."

"He started a fight."

"A riot. He stood up on the bar and shouted, 'Long live the Queen and I can whip any man's ass in the joint!' Then he proceeded to do it."

By now Carter had his head in his hands. "How much were the damages?"

"Five thousand, I think."

"Is there a phone?"

She pointed. Carter had to go through three people before he got an official who would confirm that, if the damages and court costs were paid, Smiley Lassiter would be released.

"Thank you. Would it be possible to speak to him?"

Two minutes later the familiar voice was on the line. "Lassiter here."

"Smiley, it's Nick Carter."

"Nick, lad, bloody marvelous to hear your voice! Where are you?"

"In your mansion."

"That so? Met Barbara, have you? Cheeky thing but sweet, really. Are you on holiday?"

"No, business."

"Really. I say, you wouldn't have a file you could slip me, would you?"

"No, but I may have five thousand dollars."

"Is that what the bloody wimp wants? God, I only wrecked one room."

"Smiley, listen. It's south, and the fireworks will be very bright."

"How long?"

"In and out in a week . . . if we get out."

"That touchy, eh?"

"That touchy," Carter replied. "Pays twenty-five and expenses."

"Would that be dollars, old man?"

"It would."

"Then if you'll advance five, I'd love to join the party."

"Soon," Carter said, and hung up.

Barbara intercepted him before he got to the door. "Since you're a mate of Smiley's, could you gimme a few quid . . . just to run the house on?"

"What's the name of the restaurant on Fortuna Bay?"

"Surfside."

He pressed a hundred into her hand and headed for his car.

He hit a bank, used his letter of credit, and headed to the end of the island and Fortuna Bay.

The Surfside was easy to find. There was a dark-skinned beauty with big eyes and a wide smile at the desk.

"I'd like to see the manager."

"That would be Mr. Davis-George. Whom shall I say?"

"The man with the money," Carter replied.

She looked perplexed, but glided away. In two minutes she was back. "This way, please."

The mention of money, Carter thought dryly, *works anywhere.*

The office was large and well appointed. The desk matched the room, and other than the usual accouterments it was bare and as neat as a pin.

A tall, spare man with a beetle brow and hawklike eyes stood and extended his hand. "I am George Davis-George. And you, sir?"

His accent was London-Cambridge old school and his manner was haughty and stuffy. The Killmaster decided not to mince words or time. As he spoke he arranged five neat piles of one-hundred-dollar bills on the desk between them.

"I understand a man named Lassiter caused some disruption in your establishment the other evening."

"Are you Mr. Lassister's solicitor?"

"No, I'm not, Mr. Davis-George, and my name is of no importance. What is important is your estimate of the damages. The police have informed me that the figure is five thousand dollars."

"That is correct."

"Here is your five thousand dollars. I would appreciate it if you would accompany me to the police and sign a release for Mr. Lassiter."

"I'm afraid I can't do that."

"You what?"

"I can't do that. The damages must be paid, yes. But the man's a menace. He must be punished."

Carter stood, sat on the edge of the desk, and leaned toward Davis-George.

"I don't think you quite understand. You're getting your money."

"Quite, but I also want satisfaction in seeing that man—"

"Sir," Carter said in a low voice, interrupting him, "Smiley Lassiter is a fun-loving man who sometimes drinks too much. Now, when he does that he develops a bit of a mean streak. But I'm telling you, sir, his mean streak with several drinks is nothing compared to mine with one drink. Now, you pick up that money and find your car and follow me to the police or you'll find out that the damage Lassiter did is like a drop of rain in a golf-ball-sized hailstorm compared to what I'll do."

By the time Carter stopped talking the man's face was flushed and his hands were shaking.

But it took him only a few seconds to make up his mind. He scooped the money into a drawer, and a half hour later they were springing Smiley Lassiter.

Estrella Gomez met him at the airport in Tangier with a rental car.

"God, you look like hell."

"I've been sleeping on airplanes. Did you get me a room?"

"I've got a two-bedroom suite," she replied, steering the car expertly through traffic. "I thought it would be more convenient."

Carter didn't comment on that. "Are we any closer?"

"Much. There's an old underworld character from Marseille. Evidently he's been bankrolling Namali until he can get his own setup going here. His name is André du Farre. I'm meeting someone this afternoon who can put me on to du Farre."

"Have you put out the word that we want Namali for a paying job?"

"Sure, but they aren't biting. Evidently the police have used the same trick."

"This afternoon, you say?"

"Yes."

"Good," Carter replied, yawning. "I'll get some sleep."

And sleep he did. It was dark when his eyes popped

open to find Estrella sitting on the side of the bed shaking him.

"God, you can sleep."

"It's easy when I know someone like you is watching over me," he chuckled. "What time is it?"

"Eight o'clock. I've got an address on du Farre."

Paying no attention to his nudity, Carter hopped from the bed and headed for the bath. "Rustle me up a large steak if you can find one around here."

"This is a class establishment. You can get anything your palate desires at the Les Almohades," she replied, and then grinned. "You know what, Carter?"

"What."

"You've got nice buns."

He showered, shaved, and climbed into a clean set of clothes. The steak, trimmings, and a bottle of wine awaited him in the sitting room.

He ate while she talked.

"At one time, du Farre was a big-time smuggler, did the bit from Gibralter with boats."

"Bills of lading for Cyprus and Malta, only the goods were landed in Spain," Carter said.

"You got it. Well, he's semiretired now, but he sets up for others. He also handles and launders money. Evidently he's something of a financial genius."

"Where do I find him?"

"Lives a quiet life about five miles out of the city. His villa is called the Sparrow's Nest."

Carter used the little Seat she had rented.

The Sparrow's Nest was one of a long line of sumptuous villas along the coast. Each of them sat on about three acres of immaculately tended lawn. The gate was invitingly open, and Carter drove in.

The door was answered by a small, plump woman in a tentlike white djellaba.

"Yes?"

"I would like to see Monsieur du Farre."

"He has retired for the night."

"This is very important . . . business."

"He can see no one at this—"

Carter started in, when the woman was replaced by two very large, very mean-looking gentlemen.

"Go away," one of them growled.

"Quickly," said the second.

They undoubtedly thought their sheer weight and ugliness would scare him off. That gave him the advantage of surprise.

Carter didn't chance Number One's flat belly or heavy jaw. He hacked the man across the throat, but not too hard, only enough to paralyze the vocal cords temporarily.

Then he used his shoe and kicked Number Two in the kneecap. As he was going down, Carter broke his nose with a lifting knee.

While the two of them writhed on the floor, Carter turned to the wide-eyed woman. "Now, if you'll be so kind as to take me to Monsieur du Farre . . ."

"That won't be necessary."

He was a dapper little man, not more than five feet tall, dressed in a crimson smoking jacket and gray slacks. His hair was stark white, and he sported a Vandyke beard and mustache to match.

"I imagine you have something to do with the woman who has been trying to locate myself or Mohammed Namali for the past two days?"

"You imagine correctly."

"Come into my office."

Carter followed him from the hall through a living room whose walls were hung with expensive oil paintings. There was an outsize abstraction in the gigantic room that cut it off from the dining section. Other paintings, all of them looking well cared-for, graced the walls. Halfway across the living room area was a small bookcase, a bar back-to-back with a striped sofa in red and white, and four chairs set around a cocktail table that looked like a turtle.

From the house and the man himself, Carter guessed that André du Farre was a class act.

"Would you care for a drink?"

"Scotch, one cube. Sorry about your friends."

"No matter," he shrugged, fixing the drink with a flourish. "That's what they get paid for. Besides, I admire your tenacity. We have been watching the woman. I rather expected she would make a contact eventually. If you hadn't arrived at the airport this morning, I would have probably had her picked up tonight for a little chat. Here you are."

Carter accepted the drink. "*Santé*."

"Cheers. What do you want with Mohammed Namali? I assume, by your actions, that you are not police."

"No."

"Then who are you?"

"For several reasons I have to remain a free-lancer."

"With no name?"

"Mohammed knows me."

"But you want no one else to know you. That's why the young lady used no names in looking for Namali."

"Exactly," Carter said, nodding. "Now, where can I find him?"

"Soon enough. I assume that you want to hire him for . . . some project?"

"A fair assumption."

"I see. Well, I am what you might call an agent for Mr. Namali's talents."

"So you get a cut."

"Quite."

"A week's work, twenty-five thousand."

"Out of the question. Fifty is his minimum."

"Thirty," Carter said.

"Forty."

"Thirty-five and he supplies his own materials."

"It's a bargain. You have a list?"

Carter made a hurried list of the explosives they would need. Du Farre scanned it quickly, and smiled.

"Not too difficult at all. Where would you like them delivered and when?"

"Day after tomorrow, Oaxaca, Mexico. A man by the name of Jeeter Ferris will pick them up."

"Shouldn't be too difficult." Du Farre consulted a notebook. "Have your Mr. Ferris contact a Juan Borges at the Oaxaca plant of Mexico City Ceramics. I think he'll find everything in order."

It was Carter's turn to smile. "It's nice doing business with you, Monsieur du Farre."

They shook hands and the little Frenchman lifted a phone. "Namali has a female companion. She will know where he is." He held the phone away from his ear so Carter could hear the other end.

"*Oui?*"

"This is du Farre. Let me speak to him."

"He is at The Rock with his whores. He said he would be there until midnight."

"*Merci.*" Du Farre hung up and faced Carter. "The Rock is a very disreputable place on the Casablanca highway about twenty miles south of Tangier. Alas, I fear Mohammed likes that sort of thing."

"I'll find it," Carter said.

"I'm afraid I can't phone ahead and pave your way. He will take no calls there or anywhere. It's sad, but the police used very devious methods, even going so far as saying they are me."

"Damn," Carter chuckled, "what's the world coming to?"

"Of course, you know we don't have a deal unless Namali agrees."

"Of course," Carter said, and headed for the door.

"One other thing . . ."

"Yes?"

"If there is anything else I can help you with . . . my voice reaches very great distances."

Carter paused, thinking, eyeing this little man with the gentleman's air and the challenging smile.

"There may be at that." He rifled through the photos and dossiers in his pocket, and set Venezzio on the desk in front of du Farre. "He's supposed to be dead, but I think there's a ninety-percent chance he's alive, and probably in Italy or France, or some Spanish-speaking country."

"This man Venezzio . . . he is worth a great deal of money?"

"A very reasonable sum," Carter replied.

"I'll see what I can do."

"I'll be in touch."

The old lady in the white djellaba was ministering to the two hardcases as Carter passed through the foyer. Neither of them looked at him as he went out the door.

He took the mountain road around Tangier, passed through a small stretch of desert, and hit the main highway about five miles south of the city. At this time of night it was deserted other than a few trucks and some taxis taking thrill-seeking tourists to the more disreputable clubs like The Rock.

It wasn't hard to find. A Vegas-style neon announced it from over a mile away in the dark night. Carter tipped an old car guard to watch the rental, and went inside.

To the left was a small, illegal casino. To his right was the nightclub half. A bar covered one entire side of the room, a stage the other.

The minute he hit the room Carter was aware that he had been there before. It might not have been called The Rock, but there were a hundred other places just like it all along both sides of the Med. As long as the places they were in didn't adhere too strongly to Islamic law, the booze could flow.

Three statuesque strippers were posing as belly dancers on the stage. As Carter moved toward the bar, they had already peeled down to nothing but jeweled G-strings. Those were soon tossed into the air as the lights momentarily blacked out.

There were several boos and hisses from members of the audience who hadn't grabbed enough of a look, but Carter knew that most of them would stick around for the next performance. And the next performance would be quick in coming, although not as quick as the high-priced glasses in the room would be filled in the interim.

Carter moved slowly down the length of the bar to an open space at the end, and waited until he got a glance from the bartender.

"Whiskey . . . scotch." It came, and Carter pushed a twenty across the bar. "I want to speak to a man visiting upstairs."

The bartender was Moroccan, middle-aged, and cherubic, with two gold teeth in front. "There are several gentlemen upstairs, monsieur."

"Monsieur André du Farre sent me to this gentleman."

The Frenchman's name had clout. The bartender's eyes went up and he started polishing a glass in nervous fingers. "One moment, monsieur."

He moved away, but not before pocketing the twenty. It was more like five minutes before there was a little tug at Carter's elbow.

"You wish to visit our upstairs, monsieur?"

He turned as she crawled up on the stool next to him. She was tall for a Moroccan woman, and firmly built, her womanly roundness showing in the extra-tight skirt slit high on both sides above the knee. Her clinging, black jersey blouse was worn off the shoulders and accentuated the outthrust of her heavy breasts. Her hair was a flaming artificial red, and the face was pretty, with rather high cheekbones. She was young, not more than twenty-two or twenty-three, and her figure was spectacular. But, he guessed, by the age of thirty, it was the kind that would run to fat.

"I wish to visit one of your customers upstairs."

"Who?"

Carter leaned forward until her perfume almost blinded him. "Mohammed Namali."

She shrugged. "I know of no one by that name."

"Then call du Farre."

She was gone nearly fifteen minutes, but she was smiling when she returned. "This way."

The Killmaster followed her up a wide flight of stairs and down a carpeted hall. She stopped in front of a door, knocked twice, and walked away.

Carter moved into a plush bedroom. A hidden fixture in the ceiling provided light. A huge round bed sat in the center of the room, with a long low table beside it. On the table was a smoking water pipe, a bottle of scotch, and several glasses.

"By God, it *is* you! From André's description I thought it might be!"

Carter turned. Mohammed Namali stood to the side

of the door, a Beretta held loosely in one hand, a glass in the other.

He was a short, muscular, athletic man with a thick bull neck. He was completely bald, and his skin was so black that the light gave a blue-steel tint to it.

He came forward, his teeth blazing in a smile, and embraced Carter.

"Mo, you are the damnedest man to find," Carter said.

"Have to be, my friend. I am what you might call a very hot item right now,"

"I won't ask why. You called du Farre?"

"Yes, he told me part of it. Sit, drink, tell me the rest!" Namali said.

It took a little over an hour for Carter to give him the full details of the problem. When that was done, he pulled out a map of Central America and began to outline the solution to it that he and Hawk had worked out.

When the Killmaster finished, Namali leaned back with a sigh and poured three fingers of fresh scotch into his glass.

"It is, my friend, a lot more difficult than robbing banks."

Carter chuckled. "It is that. That is also why your fee is generous."

"Who else is involved in this?"

"Jeeter Ferris is handling the arms and getting them in. Smiley Lassiter will pose as a Bell representative from London. He'll steal the chopper and fly us out. Jake Tory will run the ground operation on-site."

"Lassiter and Jake Tory I know."

"Jeeter's a good man," Carter said. "And he knows the area like the back of his hand."

"Okay," Namali sighed. "Then the big holdup, as I see it, is finding Ramón Baldez in the first place."

"State is working with someone on the inside now. Her name is Dominique Navarro. She's close to the government, so there's a good chance she may find out where Ramón is being held. I also have an ace of my own."

"The Vargas woman?"

Carter nodded. "Between them, I think we have reason to believe that we'll get the location."

"And if we don't?"

"Then, Mo, my friend, we are in deep shit. But that's why we don't work for minimum wage. Are you in?"

"Hell, yes," Namali said. "It sounds like a good party! One small hitch, though. I have a bit of a problem traveling right now."

Carter freshened his own drink. "Can you get to Gibraltar?"

"Yes."

"Then do it, tonight. You'll fly out tomorrow morning on a British passport."

Namali held up his glass. "Nick, I admire your style. Would you like a little fun and games tonight before we venture forth into the breach?"

"No, thanks," Carter said and grinned. "Just finding you took all the energy I had left for this twenty-four hours."

"Suit yourself."

Carter drove back to Tangier and the Les Almohades in high spirits. It was a good team, just about perfect. If any group could spring Ramón Baldez, this one could.

He let himself into the suite in an ebullient mood, and was a bit disappointed when the door to Estrella's bedroom was closed.

THIRTEEN

Carter checked into the Hotel Camino Real in Guatemala City and picked up a message for Mr. Jules Blackmer.

It was from the State Department man, John Fuller, and it wished him the best of luck in securing the ore options his company needed so badly.

In the privacy of his room, Carter broke it down. The gist of the decoded message was that Fuller had contacted Dominique Navarro. The woman had pledged her full cooperation and would be in contact with him as Blackmer. There was also a phone number, but it was stressed that the woman would make the first contact.

She had not been told the plan, only that Mr. Blackmer was a free-lancer who was coming in to scout the situation. Fuller had also asked her to do the best she could to find out where Ramón Baldez was being held.

Carter burned the message, hoping deep down in his gut that Fuller didn't tell the Navarro woman too much. According to her record she could be trusted, but the fewer people who knew the whole story the better.

He scrubbed the travel grime off and had a bite in his room through the first three o'clock time period. When it came and went without a call, he stretched out and slept until seven. Then he ordered a double aperitif, and after it came he drank and dressed until the eight o'clock time period.

He had told Morales that he would be coming in under an alias, so he could only hope that the old man and Lupe Vargas had enough faithful friends left in the capital to have someone spot him when he checked in.

The phone rang at exactly eight sharp.

"Yes?"

"Eleven . . . the cantina."

It was a woman's voice, but not Lupe's, and those were the only words she said.

Carter rigged Wilhelmina to his leg, settled Hugo on his right forearm, and pulled on a tropical-weight jacket. He was just walking out the door when the telephone rang again.

"Yes?"

"Mr. Blackmer?"

"Yes."

"Call me from the pay phone in the lobby."

Another woman's voice and another swift hang-up. But Carter was pretty sure he knew who this one was.

In the dining room he ate a light dinner and paid for it with a large bill. When he got his change he found the pay phone in the lobby and dialed the number Fuller had given him.

"Hello?"

"This is Blackmer."

"My name is Dominique Navarro. I assume our mutual acquaintance has contacted you?"

"He has. Can we meet?"

"It is a short drive to San José Beach. Shall we say a swim at ten tomorrow morning?"

"Fine."

"I'll be wearing—"

"I've seen your picture," Carter interrupted. "I'll know you."

He went into the lounge and ordered a brandy. The

place was as dark as night and crowded. It took him several minutes before he spotted Smiley Lassiter's tall frame and cheerful face. He was regaling two very young, very pretty girls with all the reasons why they should share his bed that night.

Carter was pleased with his appearance. He looked like an overage hippie in tight blue jeans and a torso-fitting T-shirt with the name of an American beer printed across the front of it. The label was distorted by his bulging pectorals.

Their eyes met, held for a brief second, and then broke.

Five minutes later, Lassiter excused himself to the girls. He was scarcely out the door when Carter moved to the end of the bar. There were two phones. One was a house phone with no dial. The other had a dial for direct outside calls.

"Use the phone?" Carter asked the bartender lounging nearby.

"There is a pay phone in the lobby, señor."

"I know," Carter replied, sliding a large bill his way. "It's in use."

The bartender nodded, pocketed the bill, and moved away.

Carter dialed the lobby phone and Smiley picked it up on the first jingle.

"Where are you staying?" Carter asked.

"A hostel on the north end of town. Lots of kids studying the terrible plight of the locals in between getting drunk and laid."

Carter chuckled. "I see you're not doing too badly in that department."

"Part of my cover, old boy."

"Did you get a look?"

"That I did. The airfield is nothing. Security is terrible. Without trying, I got within fifty feet of a maintenance shed today.''

"Okay, you've got your other papers?''

"I do. Quite good forgeries, too.''

"Stay with the hippie bit until I give you the word. I assume you brought some executive-type clothes?''

"Of course. When do we contact again?''

"Five tomorrow afternoon, same way.''

"Good enough. Cheerio.''

Carter left another bill on the bar for his brandy, and walked out. He passed Lassiter coming in, but neither man's eyes met.

In the street he hailed a taxi, rode a few blocks, got out, and hailed another. He used all the time until a few minutes before eleven making sure he didn't have a tail.

By then he was across town in the older section of the city where he knew the Blisters cantina would be. A late-closing news vendor gave him the exact directions, and Carter walked the remaining distance.

It was a joint in every sense of the word. B-girls flitted from man to man, making dates for the evening after a drink or two was consumed. One of them, a tiny, doll-like creature, eyed Carter as he moved to the bar. He returned her stare, then broke it to order a beer.

When he saw her again she was working a new mark two tables from him. The guy was pawing her openly, and through it all she smiled. She also deftly picked his pocket, disappeared into the ladies' room with the wallet, then reappeared two minutes later to plant the empty wallet back in the man's pocket.

She let him paw her for a minute or two longer, and then moved on to greener pastures.

Eventually she worked her way onto the stool beside Carter. "Buy Rosa a drink?''

Carter nodded, and a tall glass was in front of her

before the movement stopped.

The routine with Carter was the same as the man at the table. She took both his hands and placed them on her breasts. In a cooing voice she encouraged him. At the same time, she leaned forward and Carter could feel her talented fingers working inside his jacket while her lips nibbled at his ear.

Suddenly she leaned back and flung his hands from her breasts. "Oh, you cheap, cheap! Rosa would never make love for twenty dollar!"

She flounced off the stool and away. Carter waited a few minutes and slid his wallet far enough out of his pocket to see the end of the piece of paper she had slipped in among the bills.

He paid for the drinks and read the note outside on the sidewalk: *Next door. Jubal's. Choose Miranda.*

That was confusing until he looked at the sign: Jubal's was a massage parlor.

He had scarcely hit the door when he heard a little bell ring somewhere and four girls filed into the tiny vestibule.

"Good evening," said the first, "I am Maria."

All four of them introduced themselves. Miranda was the last in line, a tall young woman with hair the color of copper, a flat face, and onyx eyes.

Carter chose Miranda. She stepped forward, took his hand, and led him through a beaded curtain. They went down a dark hall with doors, some open, some closed, on either side. She stopped at the end, by a narrow stairway leading to the second floor, and went into a room.

"Thirty dollars."

Carter paid her.

"Take off your clothes. Lie on the table. Wait."

She left. The Killmaster stripped and lay down on the table, with the Luger under the small pillow.

Behind him he heard the door open and close. Then he felt a hand touch his back and slide up between his shoulder blades to his neck.

"Did you have a good trip?"

There was no mistaking the low, sultry voice. Carter rolled over and looked up at Lupe Vargas's smiling face.

"Very," he said, and brought her face down to his. The kiss was full of warmth but very little passion. He sensed she wanted to talk.

"What have you found out?"

"They have Ramón Baldez in the north, somewhere around Caban. We learned this because they brought him in at night. The terrain is dangerous to fly through by night, so they landed at Caban and went overland into the mountains by jeep."

"But you don't know exactly where?"

"Not yet. Morales is up there now, moving through the villages, asking about a jeep caravan passing through. I should know by midday tomorrow. How do we get him out?"

Quickly, Carter filled her in on the man he had recruited and the basic tenet of the plan. She nodded agreement at each point, and when he was finished, she sighed with relief and sat on the edge of the table.

"It sounds good. I only hope I am doing the right thing."

"You are," Carter said. "Are you safe?"

"I am." She smiled. "I didn't realize how many friends I still had in my country."

Carter ran his finger down the strong line of her jaw. "Let's hope, when this is all over, that you can stay in your own country."

Suddenly her arms went around him, holding him

tight. She kissed his cheeks. Carter combed his fingers in her thick dark hair and their lips came together.

This time the kiss was full of passion.

"Is that door locked?" Carter murmured.

"Yes."

They kissed again, lips open, her tongue touching his. He pulled her into him so that he could feel her breasts against his bare chest. A zipper ran down the back of her dress. He pulled it from neck to waist.

Her eyes grew glassy as they kissed and he tugged the dress from her shoulders.

"Should we . . . ?" she whispered.

"We should," Carter replied.

He undid the hooks of her bra and let it fall away from her jutting breasts. They came alive in his hands and the nipples seemed to search for his lips.

"I will contact you at the hotel, tomorrow, as soon as I know." Her voice had grown even lower, more husky.

"Just be careful," he said, his hands moving down her bare flesh to her hips.

He curled his thumbs under the dress and panties and peeled them down over her hips. When they fell to the floor he ran his hand gently up between her thighs. He held her there, hearing her breath catch in her throat.

Then he lifted her to the table and covered her body with his.

"This isn't right, you know . . ."

"Why not?" he replied in a hoarse whisper.

"It's thirty dollars for a massage. This is extra."

Carter chuckled as he moved his hips between her thighs and felt her hands find him. "We'll charge it to Ramón Baldez."

The truck was loaded with white wooden crates, and

the sign on the door read MEXICO CITY CERAMICS. It was a familiar sight on the road from Oaxaca to the port city of Salina Cruz.

Six miles from the ocean, Juan Borges pulled into a roadside comfort station. He parked right beside an old broken-down pickup truck and killed the engine. With a groan, he slouched casually out of the cab and walked behind the cardboard shield where truckdrivers relieved themselves.

He took longer than usual. Far longer. When he reappeared and returned to his truck, he checked the light chains that held the crates in place and grunted in satisfaction.

Two crates from his truck now rested under the tarpaulin of the pickup, but the man who had shifted them had tightened the chains back expertly.

Juan Borges got back in his truck and pulled out onto the highway.

The pickup waited a full fifteen minutes, and then it, too, pulled out onto the highway.

Jeeter Ferris drove at a steady fifty-mile-per-hour pace to the outskirts of Salina Cruz. He turned off the main street and slowly rolled along until he spotted the mouth of a narrow alley.

About a hundred yards down the alley he rolled to a halt behind a small, paint-peeling house. Outside the pickup, he took a quick glance at an unlighted window, flipped his cigarette away, and mounted the rickety steps.

The door opened easily under his hand. This was always the worst part. The hair prickled on the back of his neck as he pushed the door open very slowly. It swung back in the darkness and he waited, his senses alert and his heartbeat accelerating.

"Manuel . . . ?"

A penlight flickered on and darted across his face before it went out.

"Shut the door." Jeeter closed the door and flipped the lock. The penlight came back on, its beam on the floor at Jeeter's feet. "In here, the other room. There are heavy curtains at the windows."

Jeeter followed him into the other room. The moment the door closed, a wall switch was flipped and the room was bathed in light.

Jeeter blinked his eyes several times. When they adjusted he saw a creaking wooden bed, a few chairs, a dresser with its mirror cracked, and six rectangular boxes on the floor at the foot of the bed.

"Did you get it all?" Jeeter asked.

"All but the mines," the man called Manuel said. "They are hard to come by these days, and even harder to transport."

The man, Manuel, moved to the boxes and began prying their lids with a crowbar. He was a squat, broad man wearing a rumpled, soiled white suit with an incongruous flower in the buttonhole.

Jeeter Ferris had been buying smuggled arms from him for years, mostly for the illegal collectors' market in the States.

"This is the biggest shipment you've ever called for," Manuel commented as he worked.

"It's been a while between orders," Jeeter said, and knelt to examine the contents of each box as it was opened. In his mind he ticked off the memorized list as he went.

Two .3 Browning light machine guns, each with four thousand rounds.

Five Kevlar body armor vests.

Six Soviet 9mm Stechkin pistols.

Six Kalashnikov AK-47 assault rifles with ammo.

Each of the rifles was also rigged with a grenade launcher. One entire box was filled with spare ammo and both fragment and SAS-style flash grenades.

"Satisfied?" Manuel asked, showing the webbed patterns of laugh lines at the corners of his eyes and mouth.

"As always," Jeeter Ferris replied, passing the man a thick envelope. "Let's get it all on the pickup."

"Where is the boat?"

"Dolpho Village, in the marina."

Manuel nodded. Dolpho was down the coast about four miles from Salina Cruz. It was a favorite spot for fishermen because they could get in and out without fighting the heavier sea traffic at Salina Cruz.

It took a half hour to load and another half hour to bypass the city and drive into Dolpho.

The village center was marked by a dusty, dry fountain with a headless statue. A Catholic church stood on one side of the square, a communal bath and cantina on the other. The town market was empty, and a lone, sleepy-eyed policeman in a rumpled, dirty uniform lounged in front of the civic building.

Both Jeeter and Manuel waved to the policeman, who waved back.

Ten minutes later they were at the pier. Carrying together, it didn't take long to transfer all the boxes from the pickup to Jeeter's boat, the *Hot Tamale*.

"Ceramics?" Manuel asked, gesturing toward the two largest crates.

"That's how your stuff gets into the States," Jeeter lied.

The old man left in the pickup, and Jeeter killed the lights in the main cabin. Then he dug out a bottle of Jack Daniel's and sat down to wait.

It was almost two in the morning when he heard

footsteps on the dock and then a whispered call, "Ahoy, *Hot Tamale!*"

Jeeter stepped out on deck. A stocky black man stared up at him with a gleaming smile.

"Ahoy yourself. You don't look like an Arab."

"Half," came the amused reply. "My mother was Senegalese."

"Come aboard."

Mohammed Namali climbed up the ladder and dropped to the deck with an extended hand.

Jeeter took it. "Jeeter Ferris."

"Glad to meet you. We're supposed to check in from Mapastepec Beach around two tomorrow afternoon. You know it?"

Jeeter nodded. "There isn't much about the Mexican coastline on this side I don't know. It's about two hours to the frontier from there. Drink?"

"Love one."

The two men went below and killed the rest of the bottle of Jack Daniel's before sacking out for the rest of the night.

FOURTEEN

Carter passed through San José at nine-thirty and drove the mile or so on out to the beach. He parked above the seawall and stripped down to sweat shirt, swimsuit, and sandals.

Then, carrying lighter and cigarettes in a towel, he locked the car and walked across the sand.

It was a perfect morning for a swim, the Killmaster thought as he picked a spot and peeled off his sweat shirt. Even though the hour was early, there were already a lot of bathers. The water was clear and like glass except for two speedboats racing one another and kicking up twin foaming wakes a couple of hundred yards offshore.

Carter arranged the towel, sat, and lit a cigarette. He scanned the beach and diving raft offshore. There was a couple on the raft. The woman was leggy, full-figured, and dark-haired. Because of the distance, Carter couldn't get a clear shot of her face, but he canceled her anyway. It was a pretty sure shot that Dominique Navarro wouldn't bring a boyfriend along to meet him.

The only other woman who might fill the bill was about twenty-five yards to his left, lying on a striped towel. She wore only the bottom half of a bikini and she lay with her head on her forearm, her face turned the other way.

He was about to approach her, when she lifted her head and turned to face him. The face did not match the body, and it was definitely not Dominique Navarro.

He finished his cigarette and lay on his elbows soaking up the sun. The speedboats still played and the couple left the raft. They reached the beach and turned toward a combination boathouse and restaurant to Carter's right.

Idly he followed their progress, and then came alert. A tall, striking woman with long black hair emerged from the dressing area of the boathouse and walked to the end of the pier. As she pinned up her hair she looked down the beach.

The Killmaster stood, facing her. It was quite a distance, but from the way her body language angled toward him, Carter had a gut feeling that she was the one.

He went splashing off into the water. It was probably with a little too much bravado, he thought, because, when he hit it, he found its coldness quite a shock. But as he swam out toward the raft he got used to it and felt clear-headed and refreshed.

The raft was still empty as he climbed the ladder. He stood there for a moment and let the water drop from his body to the bleached white canvas. He surveyed the sparkling water and slowly turned to take in the beach.

Then he looked toward the boathouse again.

He could see her approaching the raft, face framed in a white bathing cap, arms and legs churning the water in a twelve-beat Australian crawl.

She reached the ladder and swung onto the raft, lissome in a figure-hugging one-piece suit. Even before she took of the cap and shook out her glossy black hair, Carter knew who she was.

"It's a beautiful morning for a swim," he said, lying down on the canvas.

"But only in the sea," she replied, stretching out beside him. "Jules, isn't it?"

"That's right. Your pictures don't do you justice."

He watched as little streams of water ran from her olive-toned skin to puddle on the canvas. She had a perfect, compact body of flowing, rounded curves, from her melon-shaped breasts to her narrow waistline that spread to round, compact hips and exquisite legs. Their heads were close together and remnants of her scent wafted to his nostrils from her hair when she removed the bathing cap. It was an expensive scent he couldn't place.

She ignored the compliment. "Why are you here?"

He shrugged as he came up on one elbow to watch her eyes and facial reactions to what he said. "Just to assess the situation."

"For whom . . . Fuller?"

"Partly. Let's just say I'm kind of like a U.N. delegation of one. Have you been able to locate where they are holding Baldez?"

Her eyes opened and bored into his. "The situation in my country is volatile, very volatile. President Baldez took another turn for the worse last night."

"All the more reason Ramón Baldez must be kept alive."

"General Cordovan is in constant contact with the rebels. He is paying the ransom this morning. With any luck, the younger Baldez will be released soon afterward. So you see, Jules Blackmer, there is very little we can do."

"Maybe not. But then, maybe there is. Do you know where the transaction is taking place?"

"The money is being transferred to a bank in the Cayman Islands. When that is done, Esteban Vargas has assured the general that Ramón Baldez will be released."

Carter paused, his mind racing. He had little doubt now that Cordovan was behind it all. He was setting up the dead Vargas to take the fall for Ramón Baldez's death. And, along the way, pocketing a very healthy hunk of the country's treasury.

"What if I told you that I don't think the rebels have Ramón Baldez?"

Her reaction was normal . . . shock, surprise. But Carter also thought he spotted a little fear in the way her flashing emerald eyes suddenly grew wide.

"I don't understand. If Vargas doesn't have the president's son, who does?"

"Good question, but it could be Cordovan himself."

The eyes grew even wider. "Impossible."

"Not really." Carter reiterated all that had happened, and summed it up as pointing to a bid for full power by Cordovan once the old president was dead.

She grew very thoughtful and eventually nodded. "It is possible, I suppose."

"I think it might even be probable." Carter almost told her that he knew Esteban Vargas was already dead, but, at the last second, held back. There was no sense involving Dominique Navarro beyond using her to get information. "Have you any idea where Ramón Baldez is being held?"

"As you know, I am not close to General Cordovan. He is acting head of the country now, so I don't have the source of knowledge I once had. But I still have contacts."

"You're not answering my question," Carter growled.

"It's somewhere in the north. I think I can tell you by evening. But I want to know one thing . . ."

"Yes?"

"I want to know what you plan to do."

Carter hesitated again, and then decided he owed her that much. "I'm going to rescue him."

"You? One man?"

"I'll have help," Carter replied. "What happens after he's free is up to the people of your country, but I think they should have a choice."

She seemed to mull this over, and then made up her mind. "All right, I will contact you this evening."

She stood and Carter joined her. She flicked the bathing cap in the air to balloon it out, and then tugged it over her head.

They dived from the raft together. As he came to the surface of the water he saw her quite a distance in front of him. She was a strong swimmer, and she wasn't wasting any time getting to shore.

And then he heard it, the powerful roar of one of the speedboats. It was coming from the right and bearing down directly on her bobbing white cap.

"Dominique! Dominique, look out!" Carter shouted.

She didn't hear him. He surged after her, his long, strong arms cutting the water and his legs beating out a powerful rhythm. But he couldn't close the gap. In fact she was gaining, and so was the speedboat. Over her head Carter could see people on the beach. They were waving and shouting at the driver of the boat, who apparently couldn't hear over the roar of the powerful engine.

The boat was only about twenty yards from the woman when suddenly it veered. The engine stalled for a second as the bow raised high in the air.

And then it slapped the water again, heading directly for Carter.

The Killmaster lifted himself from the water and waved his arms. It did no good. In avoiding the woman the boat driver had not seen the second swimmer.

There was no time to dive. As the bow charged toward him, Carter did the only thing he could do.

He kicked as hard as he could, lifting himself out of the water. At the same time, he threw himself to the side so that the deadly curve of the boat's bow would miss him.

He screamed in pain as the hull raked his chest, but by pushing off at the same time with his hands he was able to avoid being cut in half.

Nevertheless, the blow was solid. He felt as though his ribs had been caved in and he couldn't make his arms or legs work.

He felt himself sinking, with his chest screaming both from the blow and the need for air. Just as he felt blackness overcoming him, he also felt two pairs of strong hands beneath his armpits, tugging him to the surface.

He gasped for air as his head came up. It burned his lungs, but at least he was breathing. He felt himself being towed and then lifted. Then his back was on the warm sand and delicate fingers were running along his rib cage.

"Damned fool, coming in that close to shore!"

"Did anyone get the marina number?"

"Didn't see one."

"Where did he go?"

"Up the coast. He probably didn't even know he hit someone!"

Carter blinked his eyes open. They focused on

Dominique Navarro's beautiful face. Over her shoulder he could see two heavily muscled youths, their dark faces glowering.

It must have been these two who pulled him out, Carter thought.

"Are you all right?" she asked. "There doesn't seem to be anything broken."

"I'm okay," Carter groaned, managing to sit up. "*Gracias*."

The two boys nodded, and gradually the crowd started to disperse.

"You were almost killed," she said.

"Yeah, so were you. Did you get a look at the driver?"

"No," she replied.

"Did anyone follow you here?"

"No, I'm sure of it," she said, her olive skin suddenly turning pale. "Why, do you think it wasn't an accident?"

"Let's just say I'm naturally cynical. You'd better get going."

She nodded. "You're sure you can drive?"

"I'm sure. Get the location and call me as soon as you can."

She stood and, after a last long look at Carter on the sand, moved away quickly in the direction of the boathouse.

Carter watched until she was out of sight, then crawled to his towel. He painfully pulled on his sweat shirt, gathered his things, and made his way to the car.

Just as he hit the highway back to the capital, he remembered Dominique Navarro waving her bathing cap in the air before putting it on.

The pain was much worse by the time he hit the city.

It was still almost an hour before two and the first check-in, so Carter stopped at a clinic before going on to the hotel.

An X-ray showed two cracked ribs. *Great,* he thought, *and I've got miles of jungle to wade through!* He directed the doctor to tape him extra tight, paid him, and hit the hotel at ten before two.

Jeeter Ferris was right on time.

"Blackmer here."

"Our friend has arrived," Ferris replied, "and all the goods are intact."

"Good. Are you in place?"

"We are."

"Good. I'll call you there at Tee sharp."

Carter heard the connection broken at the other end, but he didn't hang up himself. Instead he held the receiver tightly to his ear and drew his thumb across the mouthpiece. The sound simulated the phone being replaced.

A millisecond later he heard the connection break at the lobby switchboard.

Just because his calls were suddenly being monitored wasn't positive reason to believe he was made. But it was enough for Carter.

He changed clothes and hit the street. In his car he drove a few blocks to a sporting goods store. There he bought a cheap set of golf clubs, shoes, and a glove. With these in the trunk, he headed for the Mayan Golf Club.

He spotted them within blocks. There were two teams, one in an old white Ford, the other in a newer model dark Chevrolet. They traded off every few blocks, but not before Carter had made them both.

Now he had no doubt that he was blown.

He got a tee time at the pro shop and turned down a

caddie in favor of a cart. He spotted them again while hitting balls on the practice range. Both cars were in the parking lot, and they were having a serious confab.

In their suits and ties they would stick out too much on the course and around the clubhouse. He was fairly sure he would be safe on the course. He was right. By the time he reached the fifth tee he was out of sight of the clubhouse and there were no other golfers in sight.

It was a par five dogleg to the right. Just around the curve in the fairway was a pond, half of which jutted into heavy woods farther to the right.

Carter drove just short of the dogleg and rode the cart to his ball. He addressed the ball and hit it perfectly. It sliced over the corner of the pond and sailed into the woods.

He pulled the cart a short distance into the woods, pocketed a second ball, and headed into the trees. Near the tail of the pond, deep in the woods, he spotted a black-suited diver emerging from the pond and crawling up the muddy bank. Attached to his belt were two bags bulging with balls.

Carter sat on a stone and lit a cigarette. He smoked until the diver plopped down beside him.

"Hello, Jake, any trouble?"

"Nah, the old boy was more than happy to let me work the course today."

"What did you give him for an excuse?"

"I'm a cheapskate. I hate to buy balls, even used ones. Told him I'd do the whole course for a third of the balls I found. He went fishing."

Carter chuckled and took out a map. "You got the jeeps?"

"One jeep, one Land-Rover. I figured the Land-Rover would be better to haul the goods. You get the locale yet?"

"No, but I'm sure I will by tonight." Carter spread the map between them. "This village, Atzalan, is about two miles on the Guatmo side of the frontier."

"Yeah."

"There's an inlet about a mile beyond the village, here. The cliffs are sheer, with a beach at the bottom. At the foot of the cliffs is a cave. It's a restaurant. There's a crane they use to lower supplies to the restaurant. Park at the top of the cliff and walk down the footpath. The restaurant should be deserted, but check it out."

"And if it's not deserted?" Jake Tory asked.

"They are innocents. We don't want anyone killed, but we don't want anyone talking, either. If there is somebody there, put 'em to sleep until morning."

"Gotcha. And we load with the crane up over the cliff?"

"Right. The signal to bring Jeeter and the *Hot Tamale* in is three longs, two shorts, two longs."

Tory repeated it, and Carter continued.

"When you're loaded, Jeeter will sail the *Hot Tamale* back to the Mexican side. He'll motor-scooter up the frontier. You'll go up this road on the Guatmo side and pick him up outside a village called Antigua Grande. You've got the compact radios?"

"I do."

"Good. Remember, they're only good up to fifty miles, and make sure you're on high ground when you use them."

"Will do. What time do I rendezvous with Jeeter at this Atzalan?"

"Think you can make it by midnight?"

Tory consulted the map again. "Shouldn't be a problem."

"Okay, you take this." Carter folded the map and handed it over. "Where's the jeep?"

"In the parking lot of the Roosevelt Hotel. I thought you'd want to be away from the center of the city." Tory handed him a set of keys. "The tag number is there."

"I'll either meet you just before dawn at Antigua Grande, or contact you by radio. Good luck."

"Who needs luck?" Jake Tory replied. "We're pros!"

Carter finished nine holes and found his car.

As he drove through the gates, the Chevrolet and the Ford were waiting. He drove slowly back to the hotel so they would have no trouble keeping up.

FIFTEEN

Dominique Navarro drove directly from the beach at San José to the Presidential Palace on the west side of Guatemala City. Without even changing clothes she went up to the president's private quarters.

The four rooms had been converted into a miniature hospital, with a round-the-clock staff on duty.

The head nurse recognized her instantly.

"Has he asked for me at all?"

"No, Señorita Navarro. There has been no change. He has not awakened at all."

"I'll be in my office for an hour or so, and then home."

"*Sí, señorita.*"

Dominique took the stairs down to the first floor and walked to the rear of the palatial mansion where her own office was located.

There were several messages, none of any importance, and she dispensed with them quickly. This done, she used the rear exit and crossed the courtyard to the presidential garrison command headquarters. Inside, she approached the orderly on duty.

"My phone is out of order. I believe General Cordovan has been trying to reach me."

"He certainly has. Something about this man Fuller with the U.S. embassy. Go right in."

Dominique knew this to be a ruse so the orderly

157

would think she was there on everyday business.

She went down the hall, knocked once on the massive mahogany door, and entered General Cordovan's opulent inner sanctum.

He was behind the desk, awaiting her. "Lock it."

She locked the door behind her and took a chair in front of the desk.

"Well?" he growled, his massive salt-and-pepper eyebrows meeting above his hawklike nose.

"I think he's American. And you were right; he's going to try and rescue Baldez."

"Alone?"

"No, he has help. How many, I don't know."

"Rebels?"

"Perhaps. I told him I thought I could give him the information by tonight."

Cordovan leaned his bulk back in the swivel chair and made a tent of his fingers in front of his face. She knew enough not to speak when he was like this, deep in thought.

"It might work out all the better," he said at last. "If Baldez is killed and it is the American's fault because they tried a rescue attempt . . ."

"I think you should kill him tonight and get it over with."

A beefy hand came down hard on the desk. "No! I do that and the Americans will only send someone else to investigate. No, I want this American involved!"

She shrugged. "What do you want me to do?"

"Tell him."

Her eyes widened. "The *truth*?"

"Yes."

"You're a fool!" she cried, leaping to her feet.

"Calm yourself, Dominique. If I am a fool, I am a cunning one. It is simple. This American, Blackmer, at-

tempts a rescue. I will reinforce the hacienda. Eduardo
and his troops will rout Blackmer, kill Ramón, and then
fade into the jungle. The ransom has been paid. I have
kept faith. Who knows? Esteban Vargas might have
kept faith and released Baldez if this stupid American
hadn't barged in.''

Dominique Navarro bit her lip. Actually, it was a
good plan, and it might work.

"You mentioned that the account number has been
paid in the Cayman Islands?''

Cordovan nodded and passed a slip of paper across
the desk. "By now the money has probably already been
transferred to your Swiss account. I pay my debts.''

He reached for the phone, dialed, and started talking
almost immediately. "He's what? . . . Oh, my God . . .
well, pull them off. That's what I said, let him run. And
that goes for anyone he might contact. You heard me,
that's an order!''

When he hung up the phone and returned his concentration to her, Dominique's eyes were blazing.

"You had him followed? Damn you, he'll be sure
that I have tricked him! That is the most stupid . . .''

As she spoke, Cordovan heaved his bulk from the
chair and walked around the desk. When he reached her
he shut off her words with a sharp slap across the cheek.

"Not half so stupid, my dear, as you having him cut
in half by that motor launch.''

"It would have been an accident!" she cried, shrink-
ing from his upraised hand.

"Perhaps," he hissed. "But one that I didn't order.''

Cordovan moved far faster than his size would sug-
gest. He hit her, again and again, flat-handed, so there
would be no marks. When he was panting with the exertion at last, he stopped.

"You will meet the American tonight, and you will

give him the exact location of the hacienda. And you will be convincing, my dear Dominique."

"Very well," she said through her tears. "But I go directly from the meeting to the airport."

He shrugged, poking a button on his desk. "Agreed. Your work, by then, will be done. You have been paid; you will be free to go." He looked at his watch. "In the meantime, we have the afternoon."

The door to the general's private quarters opened and a muscular youth of about eighteen stepped into the room. He was dressed as a steward in a white jacket.

Dominique looked from him to the general and back again. The youth smiled as he discarded his jacket.

"No! No, I won't do it!" she suddenly cried. "Tell him not to come near me! I won't . . ."

"You will, Dominique, because you have no choice. This last time, lovely Dominique, this last little entertainment . . ."

Dominique closed her eyes and willed calm to her body as the youth removed her clothes.

Carter was puzzled by the time he got back to the hotel. On the edge of the city, both of the teams trailing him fell back and disappeared. It could be, he thought, that he was getting just a taste of the surveillance all gringo foreigners get. Or it could be they knew where he was going and would simply pick him up at the hotel.

The only way he would know for sure was to wait.

There were two messages awaiting him: *Have news. Cantina. Eight.* and *Call me.*

In his room he packed everything he would need into a small gym bag. This he carried down to the car and stashed in the trunk.

He called Washington from the lobby pay phone. The

special scrambler line was picked up by Ginger Bateman on the first ring.

"Hello there, greetings from the far south."

"Well, well, he'll be glad to know you're still alive."

"And kicking. It looks like we go tonight. Meanwhile, I need info. You have a hot wire to Interpol, Hodent?"

"Don't need one. He's still here, in Washington."

"Glorious. I want you to do some tracing on substances found in that chalet where Diaz was killed. It would probably be best to check the results on the bedsheets first."

He went on telling her in detail what to look for.

"It will probably take a few hours," she replied when he was finished. "Where can I reach you?"

"You can't. I'll call you. Also, I want you to call a man named du Farre in Tangier. Tell him Namali is fine, and ask him if he has anything on our resurrected Italian."

"That's it?"

"That's it. Later, darlin'."

It was three o'clock sharp when he returned to the room. He called the desk and told them to hold all calls. Then he lay on the bed and was asleep at once.

He awakened at precisely seven o'clock. After splashing water on his face and combing his hair, he let himself out of the room. The bag with the rest of his clothes would go into the hotel storage room to be held for the unpaid bill.

He called Dominique's number from the lobby phone. She picked it up after five rings, and her voice sounded tense.

"It's me."

"I have the location . . ."

Carter put even more tenseness into his own voice. "I can't talk now. It's too dangerous."

"But listen, I—"

"I tell you I can't talk. I've had a tail on me all day."

"Damn, damn, damn," came her reply.

"Do you know the Roosevelt Hotel?"

"Yes, but—"

"Parking lot, ten o'clock. Park your car on the street. Walk to a jeep, license number 4X-11J. Get in, wait for me."

"Listen, damn you, I can't—"

Carter hung up and walked across the dining room, whistling, and turned into the gift shop.

A half hour later he emerged from the shop with both wrists smelling as if they had spent a month in a French whorehouse.

But he had the scent.

In the dining room he had a quick snack and then went to the bar. Lassiter was already there, this time by himself. Carter gave him the look. As the pilot exited the room, Carter played the same telephone game, this time with a different bartender.

"Smiley, my lad, you've seen the last of your hippie days."

"We're on?"

"We're on," Carter replied. "Dig out your best bib and tucker. I'd say make the heist around two tomorrow afternoon. You can pick up the coordinates at the post office in the morning."

"General Delivery, my name."

"So right," Carter said, and hung up.

It was seven-thirty.

He had a half hour to lose a tail before hitting the Blisters cantina, but he was pretty sure he wouldn't need it.

• • •

The only difference in the atmosphere at the Blisters cantina the second time around was the fact that it was less crowded. The bartender was still uninterested, and the B-girls still moved to the beat of money.

Chief among them was Rosa.

She spotted Carter the instant he entered, but didn't get around to him for several minutes. When she did, things were different.

Instead of going for his wallet or playing coy with her body, she went right for the jugular. Her arms went around his neck and her lips worked from ear to ear.

"You like Rosa, gringo?"

Carter went along with it. He moved his own hands under her blouse and up her back. "I like very much."

"Maybe you like to spend a little time in Rosa's room?"

"A lot of time, maybe."

"Ah, señor, Rosa is very expensive!"

This banter went on for a few more minutes, and then she slid from the stool. She took his arm and tugged him toward the rear of the place.

"Okay, gringo," she said very loudly, "c'mon, we see how good a man you are!"

They mounted a flight of stairs, went down a long, dimly lit hall, and up a second flight of stairs.

"Where are we going?" Carter asked.

"My office," she giggled.

"How many people know about this?"

"Just myself, my sister Miranda next door, and the woman who owns both places. It is safe, señor."

Her manner had radically changed, from the coquettish whore to the very practical woman.

The "office" turned out to be a garishly decorated bedroom, with lots of fringed velvet and very low lights.

Lupe Vargas awaited them.

"When you are ready to go, press this bell," Rosa said. "I'll take you through the cellar. It comes out three doors away."

"*Muchas gracias, Rosa,*" Lupe said.

"*De nada,*" the woman shrugged, and was gone.

"Do you have a map?" were Lupe's first words to Carter.

"Yes." He took a detailed chart from his inside coat pocket, a twin to the one he had given Jake Tory.

"All day yesterday and today, Morales worked westerly out of Caban—here. There are many coffee plantations in the area, and several small villages between the plantations. Here—between the two rivers—it is very rocky instead of fertile the higher you go. The place where Ramón Baldez is being kept is called the Hacienda del Campo. It is here."

Carter pinpointed the spot and figured the scale from the frontier and from Antigua Grande near the frontier.

"What do you know of it?" he asked.

"Only what Morales tells me, but he knows the area well. A rich Italian came here after the Second World War, with dreams of planting coffee above the existing land. He stole the land from the Indians and practically enslaved them. They hated him, so he was forced to make a fortress out of the hacienda. He died in the fifties, and the land and hacienda went back to nature. Few villagers go near the place. The Indians think it is protected by the ghost of its owner. Esteban's guerrillas used it for a base for a while about a year ago."

"And he probably pumped up that superstition with the natives."

She nodded.

Carter wrote the coordinates on a slip of paper and

slipped it into an envelope. He addressed it and handed
it to her. "Can Rosa put a stamp on this and get it
mailed outside the main post office tonight?"

"Yes. Nick . . ."

He frowned when he saw the look on her face. "What
is it?"

"There is something else. This morning, Morales
climbed the mountain behind the hacienda."

"And?"

"He counted twelve men guarding Baldez. He recognized their commanding officer, Eduardo Taza. They
are all in fatigues, without rank, as if they were guerrillas."

"That figures."

"And before he left, twenty more men arrived. They
made camp below the hacienda."

To Lupe's surprise, Carter only smiled at this news.

"You think reinforcements are a joke?" she cried.

"No, but you're an old guerrilla fighter. What would
you make of it?"

"I'd say it was a trap."

"Exactly," Carter agreed, nodding. "You have the
scooter?"

"Yes, parked down the alley."

"Good. I have to make a phone call to Washington
along the way, so we'll leave soon. Take the letter to
Rosa. We'll leave in a half hour. Also, how have you
been reaching Morales?"

"By phone, to someone he trusts in a village near the
lake."

"You're sure it's a safe line?"

"Positive."

"Then I'll use it too. Come get me when it's safe.
Give Morales the coordinates."

While she was gone, Carter stripped and dressed again from the small bag. All the clothes were dark: a turtleneck, a pair of jeans, a black windbreaker, and a heavy pair of boots.

Lupe returned. "Come."

"You called Morales?"

"Yes, he will get the message. In here!"

The call went through at once. Bateman had all the information he asked for, and then some.

"Du Farre is sure about Venezzio?"

"That's what he says."

"Okay. You know the hour alphabet code?"

"Sure."

"I gave Jeeter a Tee time for a call in Mapastepec, Mexico."

"Tee would be eight o'clock plus two. Ten o'clock."

"Right. Here's what you tell him . . ."

Carter gave her the coordinates, times, and the place to meet Jake Tory. When he was sure she had it all, he hung up and turned to the two women.

"Let's go!"

Carter pulled to the curb about a block from the Roosevelt parking lot and killed the scooter. There were few cars and no pedestrians.

"Wait here. When you see the jeep lights come on, follow us."

"Who is she?" Lupe Vargas asked.

"With any luck, our ticket into that hacienda."

The Killmaster climbed off the scooter and moved down the street from car to car. When he spotted a small Volvo with government plates, he stopped. The two bags resting on the rear seat brought a smile to his lips.

He moved into the parking lot and silently ap-

proached the jeep. She gasped as he yanked the door
open and slid into the driver's seat.

"Jesus, you scared the hell out of me!"

Carter didn't waste time or mince words. He laid the
map across her lap and used a penlight. "Where?"

"Here. There is an old hacienda . . ."

Carter listened in silence to the whole litany. It correlated perfectly with the information from Morales.
That is, it correlated except for the twenty or more
added troops that had moved in that morning.

When she had finished, the Killmaster smiled. He
folded the map and softened his tone. "Terrific, you're
going to be a big help."

She was reaching for the door handle. "I hope you're
successful . . ."

"With your help, I'm sure we will be," he said.

He slid his hands down her arm, arresting the movement. At the same time, he moved his face close to hers
and lightly brushed her jawline with his lips.

"I love your perfume, Dominique. 'Jadin,' isn't it?"

"Good God, what does my perfume have to do—"

"Nothing, really. It's just that so few scents come out
of Morocco. Jadin is very rare. It is Jadin, isn't it?"

"Yes, now if you don't mind—"

Carter started the jeep and screamed out of the parking lot.

"What the hell do you think you're doing?" she
cried.

"Taking you with me." In the rearview mirror he
could see Lupe Vargas fall in behind them. "Since you
use Jadin perfume, I assume you also use the rest of the
line, like the talc and body lotion."

She was getting it. Carter could tell from the contor-
tions of her face, and more of the same fear he had seen
earlier in her eyes.

Her hands began clawing at the small purse in her lap. He clutched one of her wrists and squeezed. When she screamed he released the wrist and grabbed the bag.

Inside was a little .25 automatic. Not much of a gun, but very deadly from up close.

"Interpol found traces of Jadin body powder on the sheets beside Diaz's body in Spain."

Again his fingers went into the purse, this time coming out with her passport.

"When I get a chance to look at this, I think I'll find a Spanish entry and exit stamp, and I also think the dates will match up."

Carter threw the .25 automatic out the window and jammed the jeep's accelerator to the floor. When the needle reached eighty, he turned to face Dominique Navarro.

"If you really want to, I won't stop you from jumping out."

SIXTEEN

At seven o'clock, Smiley Lassiter checked into a small hotel next to the downtown post office.

In the room, he peeled out of the scuzzy jeans and shirt and discarded them in a wastebasket. Next he showered carefully, washing the dark rinse out of his hair and restoring it to its natural sandy blond color.

After shaving meticulously, he used a blow dryer on his hair and dressed in a light tan garbardine Cardin suit. The shirt and tie were also Cardin. The loafers he took from the well-used backpack were Gucci.

The last thing out of the backpack was a brown leather briefcase. This wasn't by Gucci. It was by Hansenbell, a clever AXE technician in D.C. The case had a false top and false bottom. Both were released by pressing a metallic card to a release.

Inside the top was an Uzi submachine gun with two extra clips. In the bottom compartment was a silencer and a collapsible stock.

Lassiter checked it all and closed the sections. In the center, or actual briefcase section, was a passport, credentials identifying him as a consultant for Bell Electronics, and a request from the Guatemalan government for a thorough safety inspection of the government's seven Bell helicopters. To back this up there was also a signed order from General Emilio Cordovan that the bearer should be given all assistance possible in carrying out his duties.

Needless to say, each and every document was an AXE forgery.

Lassiter snapped the briefcase closed and left the hotel with barely a glance from the desk clerk. Across the street, he entered the post office. Three minutes later he emerged with the General Delivery letter in his pocket, and hailed a cab.

It was nine-thirty when the taxi deposited him in a small village fronting the air force base's main gate.

Lassiter decided to pause for breakfast before he began work.

They worked well as a team. By the time Carter in the jeep had rendezvoused with the three men in the Land-Rover at five in the morning, much of the initial work had been done.

Jeeter Ferris and Jake Tory had assembled the arms and filled the spare magazines. Mohammed Namali had broken down the two crates of explosives into good weights for each person's pack, and briefed the others on arming the charges.

At first light, Morales arrived. He briefed Carter and sketched out a floor plan of the hacienda.

"I was there in the old days with Esteban," the old man explained. "There is a wine cellar under this corner here. At one time I think it was also used as a kind of holding and torture chamber by old Del Campo to keep the Indians in line. I am positive that is where Ramón is being kept."

"Let's hope so," Carter said. "The last thing we want to do is kill Baldez ourselves. What about the guards at the house itself?"

"They work in four-hour shifts to stay alert. Four on the roofs, at each corner."

"That means twelve plus the officer."

"*Sí*," Morales said, nodding.

"And the reinforcements?"

"There are about twenty of them. They are spread on a line—here—about two hundred yards below the hacienda. They are well dug in. A frontal attack would be foolish."

"I can see that," Carter growled.

Morales inclined his head to the side. "Why is that woman here?"

Carter followed his gaze to where Dominique Navarro sat beneath a tree, glaring at them all.

"You know her?"

"Not her name. I have seen her twice in the camp of Esteban Vargas."

"Recently?"

"*Sí*," Morales said. "It was to her that Esteban sent Benito Venezzio when he wanted information from the capital."

"You're sure of that?" Carter asked.

"Positive. I don't like her. I told Esteban, she has the bad eye."

"You mean evil eye."

Morales shrugged. "It is the same. After Venezzio was killed, she came to the camp to see Esteban."

Carter glanced over at the beautiful but now bedraggled woman. She wouldn't meet his eyes.

He was fairly sure he had the whole picture now. Dominique Navarro had been playing both President Baldez and Esteban Vargas for quite some time, when in actual fact she had been in Cordovan's pocket all the time.

And Carter was pretty sure the reason was purely profit. He knew very few personal things about Benito Venezzio, but he was Italian, and a man.

Now, looking at Dominique Navarro, he could see how any man could fall under her spell. And, based on what he now knew, he was pretty sure Venezzio had.

"Jake?" The big man looked up from where he stood in the clearing, and trotted over. "How much longer?"

"I'd say another two hours to finish the hangar, and then a half hour to put out the guides that Lassiter can see from the air."

They were building a pull-and-trolley-rigged open-sided hangar for the helicopter from palm thatch, tree limbs, and foliage. They would also mark it from the air so that Lassiter could find it fast. After landing, all he had to do was pull one rope and the two sides of the hangar roof would fold together. The helicopter would then be hidden until the time came for the pilot to take off again and rendezvous with them at the hacienda.

Carter checked his watch and turned to Morales.

"That would put us out of here around noon. How long a march overland to the area of the hacienda?"

The old man squinted his eyes in thought before replying. "Considering we have to stay under cover all the way, I'd say we'd get there just before dusk."

"Perfect," Carter replied. "Will you give them a hand building the hangar?"

Morales nodded and jogged back to the clearing with Jake Tory. Carter moved to the Land-Rover where Lupe Vargas was working with the radio and jamming equipment. He stood at her shoulder, silently watching. Now he was seeing the other side of the woman he had first met in Aruba. She was truly in her element. Earlier he had seen her break down, inspect, and reassemble one of the AK-47s in less than two minutes. Now he could see that she was equally adept at the radio.

"How's it going?"

"Be operative in another twenty minutes," she replied. "When do you want to start jamming?"

"Not until after we've sent in our Trojan horse."

He lit a cigarette as he moved through the trees to where Dominique Navarro sat. She turned away when he crouched beside her.

"You're going to help us," he said.

"Fuck you."

Slowly, Carter laid out every scrap of evidence—both real and circumstantial—he had. He then told her what ends he had surmised from that evidence, ending with his guess that she had seduced Benito Venezzio to use him as her agent to put Cordovan in power.

"I'm also guessing that the ransom supposedly paid from the state treasury is in a bank account somewhere in your or Venezzio's name."

Dominique turned her head and spat in Carter's face.

He managed a smile as he wiped his face with the sleeve of the turtleneck. "You have one chance to spend your ill-gotten gains, lady."

She looked for a moment as if she were going to do a repeat, but then, slowly, she relaxed and he saw a flicker of interest in her eyes.

"As soon as that radio equipment is set up for travel and the hangar is built, we're getting out of here. Just before we go, I want you to get on the radio to the Presidential Palace. Part of what you'll tell them is the truth."

"And what would that be?" She was back to being the Dominique he had taken the swim with . . . cool, confident, and cunning.

"I want you to tell Cordovan that I took you with us but you still have my complete trust. You've learned my strength, and my time and plan of attack.''

"Which will, of course, be wrong.''

"Of course.''

"What happens then?''

"We have a jammer with us. As soon as I'm sure Cordovan has relayed the information to Eduardo Taza at the hacienda, I'll start jamming the government's three channels.''

The woman smiled. "You know there are no telephones at the hacienda.''

"I know.''

"And what happens to me?''

"You're free to go.''

She looked around her. "Go? Go where . . . and how?''

"When we leave, I'm going to handcuff you to the steering wheel of the Land-Rover. I'll leave instructions for our pilot to turn you loose before he leaves. The keys are in the ignition. You're free to fly away to Venezzio and your loot.''

"Just like that?''

"Just like that,'' Carter said.

"How do you know I won't trip you up on the radio?''

Carter shrugged. "A couple of reasons. If we succeed, Cordovan topples and you're safe. Two, I'll have this Luger at your head. If I don't like what you say, I'll blow you away.''

"Those are very persuasive reasons.''

"Then I assume I've got your attention?''

"Undivided,'' she said dryly. "May I have a cigarette?''

He was lighting it for her when Lupe tapped him on the shoulder.

"Can I talk to you?''

Carter rose and followed her a short distance through the trees.

"Radio working?" he asked.

"No problem, and the jammer is set up. I got the capital radio on the open band . . . the news."

"Tell me," Carter said, already knowing what she was going to say.

"President Baldez died just a few minutes ago. General Cordovan has declared himself head of the government and declared martial law."

"Damn," Carter hissed. "Let's get her on the radio fast. I only hope Smiley got to the air base a little early!"

Smiley Lassiter moved aside so the pilot they had assigned him could swing down from the chopper first. Side by side, they walked toward number six.

Getting on the base and passing through the officer in charge had been ridiculously easy with his credentials.

Since then, he had already "inspected" the first five choppers. The routine had been the same for each of them. Start rotors. Check fuel pressure, oil poundage, transmission, and hydraulic. Check radio, strobe, and anticollision lights. Then take the machine up about five feet to monitor collective lever and pedals to check the tail rotor's steering pitch.

When all the checking was done, Lassiter would order the craft back to the ground and shut down. Then the last thing he would do before sliding out the hatch was slice the three fuselage hydraulic lines with a small knife. The cuts were not clear through, just enough to weaken the hoses so that when the engines reached lift-off rpm's of 483, the lines would rupture.

Lassiter had chosen to leave choppers six and seven until last because he had already spotted the fact that

they were completely fueled and armed, right down to
the four-slot rotating rocket launchers on their skids.

The pilot had the rotors spinning steadily on number
five and they were halfway through the checklist, when
they both noticed the activity around the hangars.

Suddenly the live radio crackled and Smiley saw a
jeep head their way from the hangar.

"L-four-oh-three, conclude your test. Repeat, conclude your test. We are in a state of emergency."

"I'm sorry, señor, I must shut down," the pilot said.

"What for? We're almost done."

The pilot shrugged. "One never knows."

By this time, the jeep had pulled up alongside the
hatch and an officer was standing on the seat waving at
them.

"See what it's all about," Lassiter said. "At least I
can get the steering pitch checked."

The pilot nodded and slipped out of his seat. As he
moved toward the hatch, Smiley sat down, reaching
across to the other seat and his briefcase. In seconds he
had the Uzi out and primed.

"Señor, we must stop at once!"

"Why?"

"El Presidente has died. We are on alert. It is martial
law, and all ships must be manned and ready to take
off."

"One second . . ."

"No, señor, now!"

The pilot started forward. Lassiter hit the rotors to
full power and brought back the collective stick. The
chopper lurched to fifteen feet and inched forward in a
hover.

The pilot was momentarily knocked off balance, but
now he had a grip on the side rails by the hatch and was
about to inch forward.

"Señor, stop! You must—"

Lassiter turned sideways in the seat and leveled the Uzi at him. "Jump!"

"What? Are you mad, señor?"

"Probably," Lassiter replied. "Jump. You have until the count of three. One . . . two . . ."

Lassiter never got to three. The pilot went out the hatch at two and one millionth of a tenth.

Smiley retracted the collective lever and rammed the stick. The helicopter shot into the air. At two hundred feet he pressed the left pedal and the machine veered in a wide arc. At the same time, he activated the right sled rocket launcher.

He leveled off at two hundred feet and hovered, swinging the nose around and dipping it toward number seven, the one remaining copter on the ground that could follow him.

It was as if the man in the jeep and the pilot just climbing into it knew what was coming next. The officer dropped into the seat, threw the jeep into gear, and abandoned their duty.

Lassiter fired the rocket and bellowed, "Bingo! Look at me, Ma, top o' the world!" as he sped into the sky and away from the inferno he had created.

SEVENTEEN

Carter tramped along behind Morales, trying to fight off his weariness and the pain in his chest that had gotten worse by the mile. Carefully, ploddingly, he placed one foot in front of the other without thought.

So much so that when Morales stopped abruptly, he almost ran into him.

"What is it?" Carter asked.

"There!"

Carter gazed through the mantle of thick foliage and sensed the others crowding around.

Then his eyes adjusted and the images they saw took shape.

The setup was exactly as Morales had described it.

Dense foliage flowed up the side of the mountain under a thick awning of immense mahogany, ceiba, and cedar trees. If any of the area had ever been cleared for coffee, it could not be discerned now. The jungle had reclaimed its own.

About two hundred yards below the bare limestone peak of the mountain, the jungle started. It was here where a plateau sprawled like the lower lip of a Ubangi, and on that plateau rested Hacienda del Campo.

Morales handed Carter back his binoculars. "Follow the stream down to where the curve goes strongly to the left. That is where the second group is dug in."

Carter did so, and then saw them. There was a second plateau, about twenty feet deep, and all along it for about three hundred yards men were burrowed down into foxholes. Or at least they would be. Right now they were lounging in groups beneath shade trees twenty feet above the plateau.

"Looks like the bait worked," Carter growled.

"It did at that," Jake Tory said from his right. "Now let's just hope they keep thinkin' we don't arrive until dawn."

"Namali!" Carter hissed.

"Right behind you."

Carter handed him the glasses. "See a breach in that line you can get through after dark?"

The black man gazed through the glasses for nearly ten minutes before dropping them and winking at Carter. "Hell, yes . . . two, three places. And the hacienda itself will go like a popcorn box."

"Just be sure you stay away from that far right corner." Carter trained his glasses about forty yards in front of the front line of soldiers on the plateau. "Right about there, plant a line of booby-trap charges to cover our retreat and their advance."

The black man made an ominous growl in his throat. "It would simplify things if we had some fragmentation mines. That's a hell of a wide area."

"But we don't," Carter replied. "Can it be done?"

"Yeah, it can be done. I'll use a trip wire."

Carter shifted back to the hacienda. From the front wall he could see a steady gush of water pouring through a four-foot-diameter pipe. The stream was overflow from a small lake in the cone at the very top of the mountain. On its descent, it entered the enclave of the hacienda through a similar pipe. According to

Morales, it was the source of cooking and drinking water for the house as well as providing power for a small generator.

"Morales?"

"*Si?*"

"You're sure the upside pipe is the same size as the one on this side?"

"Positive."

Carter nodded. The water, as it gushed out, was filling about three quarters of the pipe. That would be their way in.

The Killmaster motioned them to follow, and retraced their steps fifty yards back down the trail. In a small clearing, he squatted and used Hugo's point in the dirt.

"As soon as it's dark, Namali will set his first charges—here. Morales and I will skirt the enclave and go up the mountain—here—then follow the stream down to the inside wall. Hopefully, we can time it so we go through the water chute at exactly twenty-three hundred hours. By then, Namali will have breached the lower line and be at the outside walls, setting the charges there and against the house. Any questions?"

No one spoke.

"Jeeter, Jake, and Lupe will set up the machine guns and mortars—here, here, and here. Got it?"

All three of them nodded.

Lupe Vargas spoke. "I'm more accurate with the mortar."

"Okay," Carter said, then continued. "You'll also set up three alternate positions, so you can drop back with the grenade launchers and the AKs when they zero in on your first position. Any questions now?"

Tory spoke. "Do we start the bang-bang?"

"No, everyone takes his cue off the sound of the

chopper. Hopefully, by then, either Morales or myself
—or both of us—will have gotten to Baldez. In any
event, when the chopper starts in, Namali makes things
go boom and the three of you pin down the lower guard.
We don't want them streaming up that hill. We'll probably have enough trouble with the guards already up
there."

Carter paused again and drew a small circle some
distance from the rest of the chicken scratches.

"Now comes the hard part," he growled. "On liftoff
from the enclave, Smiley will land back here. Lupe—
you, Jeeter, and Jake are going to have to move. We
hope Namali's trip-wire mines will get most of them,
but some might get through and they are going to be
right on your asses. So you get out of there, *fast.*
Everybody with it?"

There was a chorus of mumbled replies and af-
firmative nods.

"Okay. Lupe!"

The woman dragged the radio between them and got
it going. When it was crackling, she handed the hand
mike to Carter.

"Skyhawk, this is Land-Rover. Come in, over."

"You're loud and clear, Land-Rover, this is Skyhawk. I'm down and dirty."

"Did you get my package?"

"I did that, and your words. Will do."

"We go at the witching hour, Skyhawk. Over."

"The witching hour it is! Cheers to all, over."

"Fly safe. Land-Rover out." Carter handed the mike
back to Lupe. "Okay, from now on we're on the hand
radios. Let's get some rest until it's time to go."

He found a soft spot under a tree and curled up. He
was just dozing, when Lupe scooted up near him.

"I still don't trust Dominique," she whispered.

"When she's gone in the Land-Rover, she might go right to a phone."

Carter shrugged. "She might, she might not. It won't make any difference."

Lupe bit her lip. "I know the signals are jammed, but Cordovan still has two jets. If he sent them . . ."

Carter debated, and then decided to tell her.

"The jammer is in the back of the Land-Rover, right?"

"Yes."

"If Cordovan sends a jet, he'll hone in on the jammer."

Lupe Vargas shivered. "Jesus, I'm glad I'm on your side!"

Carter went through first, with Morales right behind him. They ended up in a wide basin with the water bubbling over them and flowing out the other side.

As one, they rolled out of the basin and ran across a small courtyard to the safety of an overhang and receding wall. In less than a minute they had the oilskins off the AKs and the silenced handguns.

Above them they could hear the sound of the current watch's footsteps on the roof.

"The watch about to go on will be in the kitchen eating," Morales whispered. "The off-watch could be anywhere, sleeping, roaming . . ."

"We'll hit the kitchen first," Carter replied in a low voice.

They met number one before they got past the lower level. He was sitting on a ledge of the inner courtyard, smoking and looking out across the quiet valley.

Morales and Carter split and moved to each side, prone on the stones flanking him. Carter waited for a cloud to clear the sickle moon, and signaled for Morales

to stay where he was. Then he crept soundlessly along
the low wall and put a hammerlock on the unsuspecting
guard from behind. At the same time, he brought Hugo
into play.

The man started thrashing around, kicking and trying
to shout, but Carter had a death grip on his trachea.

The stiletto went in and up between his third and
fourth ribs, and the body went limp.

"Put him in here!" Morales rasped.

There was a heavily overgrown arbor hiding two love
seats. They deposited the dead man on one of them.

"That's one," Carter growled. "Lead the way!"

They went through an alcove and down two flights of
steps to the hacienda's lowest level.

"Kitchen," Morales whispered, pointing to his right.

"Wine cellar?"

"Down those steps," the old man replied, gesturing
to the left.

They went right, and crept up to a slightly ajar door.
There was a tiny window high in its center. Both men
cautiously peered through.

Two men in fatigue trousers and green T-shirts sat
chatting and sipping coffee.

"Use the Stechkins!" Carter whispered.

"Of course."

"I'll take the one on the right."

They crouched, and on eye contact rolled through the
door. Both men fired from a one-knee position, empty-
ing their clips to be positive.

"*Madre de Dios*," Morales said, "a lot of blood."

"Too much," Carter agreed. "But there's nothing we
can do about it. C'mon!"

They doused the kitchen lights and retraced their
steps to the stairs leading down to the wine cellar. At the
bottom, there was a tiny room with a table and two

chairs. On the table was a lit oil lamp that threw eerie shadows off a steel-barred door.

There was no guard.

"Cover me!" Carter hissed.

Morales turned toward the stairs and brought up the AK as Carter moved to the door.

"Baldez . . . Ramón Baldez!" the Killmaster called.

A man emerged from the darkness between two cobweb-covered wine racks, and cautiously approached the gate. His bearded face was haggard and one side of it was covered with clotted blood. The white shirt and trousers he wore were tattered and filthy.

"Who is it?" he mumbled.

"Never mind who I am. We're getting you out of here."

"To kill me?"

"No, to make you the next president, I hope. Stand back . . . far back!"

Carter jacked a new clip into the Stechkin and emptied it into the tired old lock. The gate swung wide and Ramón Baldez emerged.

His eyes were still weary. "How can I trust you?"

"You have to," Carter said.

"How is my father?"

"He died a few hours ago."

To the younger man's credit, he took the news stoically, making the sign of the cross and following Carter to where Morales crouched.

"According to your file, your military training was air force."

"It was," Ramón nodded, studying Carter carefully.

"Can you fly a helicopter?"

"I can."

"Good," the Killmaster growled. "Let's hope you get the chance soon."

"What now?" Morales asked.

"We wait," Carter replied.

Lieutenant Eduardo Taza glanced up at the wall clock and drummed his fingers on the desk.

It was nearly midnight, and still no word from the capital. The raid was not supposed to occur until dawn, but the constant jamming since the last transmission worried him.

His orders were to kill Ramón Baldez when the first shot was fired. Now Taza wasn't so sure he should wait.

"Try again!"

The man across the room at the radio shrugged and turned back to his dials. He worked all three channels and turned back to Taza with a shrug.

"Still jammed."

"Go down and bring Baldez up!"

As the sergeant left the room, Taza pulled a magnum from his holster and checked the loads.

The helicopter was barely off the ground before Dominique Navarro had the Land-Rover started and was backing it around. She would drive south and then east to Concepción. Once there, she would abandon the vehicle and walk the two miles to the Mexican border.

She could care less who won their little war now. The money was hers, in her name, in Switzerland. Benito was waiting in Portugal. The down payment was made on the fields, the château, and the winery.

In three, perhaps four months, she would have it transferred to her name and pay it off.

Then it would all be hers.

Then she would find a way to rid herself of Benito Venezzio.

At the last second she remembered her purse. She

rummaged between the two bucket seats until she found it.

"Damn, damn, damn!" she hissed when she found that all it contained was the usual female paraphernalia. Her passport was gone.

And in the passport was the deposit receipt and the transfer number to the Swiss account.

No matter, she thought, *I can get another passport, and I have the numbers memorized.*

She put the Land-Rover in gear and roared down the jungle road.

Carter heard the booted feet on the stairs first. He motioned the other two back in silence, and crouched with his back against the wall. Sliding down on his back, he rested the long snout of the silencer on one knee.

The sergeant had just turned the corner and squared his shoulders when Carter pumped three slugs into the center of his chest.

"Let's hit the roof!"

Mohammed Namali crouched in the thick undergrowth with his hand on the pull pin. From his vantage point he could see the valley below and the walls of the hacienda.

From the pull pin in his hand, a thin wire snaked along the outer wall and foundation half the length of the house.

Sweat glistened on his black face, and his heart beat like a jackhammer.

It was a minute past midnight.

Where the hell was Lassiter?

And then he heard it, the steady *thwack, thwack, thwack* of the helicopter's rotor. The sound was quickly

followed by the thud of the mortar and the chatter of
machine guns.

Namali waited until he saw the bodies below rise in
the moonlight. They were answering fire, but they were
also moving up the hill toward the hacienda.

"This will stop that crap," Namali muttered, chuck-
ling.

He pulled the charge pin, and the night erupted.

As Namali went through the wall, he saw the lower
guard dive back into their holes.

Carter and Morales hit the roof running and firing.
They got two of the guards on the first burst.

Smiley Lassiter came in with both sets of rockets blazing. The opposite wing of the hacienda crumpled before
their eyes.

"*Madre de Dios*," Morales groaned, "I hope he
leaves enough roof to land on!"

"He will," Carter replied, watching the chopper
hover and descend. "Let's go!"

"Look out!" Ramón Baldez cried.

Slugs spit up tar and gravel in a deadly path in front
of Carter. He rolled as he heard Morales scream a curse
to his right.

Two men, still in their underwear, poured from
another stairwell to his left. They were ready to fire
another burst, and Carter knew he wouldn't be able to
get his own AK up in time.

Suddenly the rifles flew out of their hands and their
bodies pitched forward, crimson spreading across their
white undershirts.

Namali's face appeared in the doorway. "Greetings."

Carter waved and turned. Morales was hit. "How
bad?"

"Leg . . . it's all right."

"Help him!"

To the Killmaster's surprise, Ramón Baldez hefted the bigger man's bulk to his shoulders and ran for the chopper. Carter got shoulder to shoulder with Namali and they backed in behind them.

Morales and Baldez scrambled into the copter while Carter and Namali sprayed the twin openings to the roof at random.

"Get aboard!" Lassiter yelled. "Let's get the fuck outta here!"

They fired a last burst and jumped aboard. Lassiter lifted about twenty feet and whirled the nose around just as Taza and a second man appeared on the roof.

The officer had a grenade in his hand, but he never threw it.

Both men disintegrated in the explosion from Lassiter's last rocket.

The chopper heeled over and headed down the mountain. They could see Lupe, Jeeter, and Jake Tory running through the bush for their lives. Every few feet they would stop and return their pursuers' fire.

"Go off, goddamn you!" Namali screamed. "Will one of you bastards hit a trip wire?"

As if at the Arab's command, one of the pursuing soldiers hit the wire. Bodies and brush lifted into the air. They could hear the screams of agony over the whirling blades of the helicopter.

There had been eight. Now there were four.

But those four were still in pursuit, and still firing.

"Down we go!" Lassiter cried out, and the nose of the helicopter dipped.

Seconds later they were hovering just three feet off the ground.

Namali and Carter leaped through the hatch and dropped to one knee.

"Run! Run like hell!" Carter screamed, the AK in his hand spewing slugs at the four soldiers who had paused behind trees to return the fire.

Without pausing in stride, the two men and the woman dived through the hatch into the chopper.

"Get on, get on!" Lassiter bellowed, already straining at the master lever.

Carter and Namali stood on the skids, with one leg curled around a brace for balance, and continued to fire. The rotors and engine of the helicopter were screaming, and everyone aboard knew the reason why.

"Too much weight!" Lassiter yelled, his right hand trying to shove the throttle lever clear through the front of the machine.

"Lift, damn you, *lift!*" Carter hissed through clenched teeth as the clip in his AK ran dry simultaneously with Namali's.

In the trees, the four soldiers started to move forward.

Suddenly, with a last shudder, the chopper began to rise. Twenty feet, thirty feet, and then it was rolling over and gaining altitude swiftly.

"Up, up, and away!" Smiley Lassiter screamed, tipping a flask to his lips.

Captain Raul Perez cursed the sluggish controls of the old surplus American jet as he made his third pass over the ribbon of road running through the jungle below.

The homing device on his radar was still picking up a powerful signal from the jammer, but he could see nothing.

He was about to curl off and head north, when he saw

it: a gray Land-Rover just coming into a treeless stretch of road.

Perez throttled back, did a roll, and screamed down toward the Land-Rover from two thousand feet.

He sighted in and fired, at the same time bringing the jet's nose up and going into a roll. Over his left shoulder he saw the rocket make a direct hit, disintegrating the Land-Rover.

He smiled with satisfaction. The jammer was silenced.

Lassiter set the helicopter down near the village of Tapazo, forty miles inside the Mexican border.

"It's all yours," Carter said to Ramón Baldez. "Lupe and Morales will go with you. Here's where we disappear."

"Gracias, muchas gracias," Baldez said, "whoever you are."

"You've got more than enough gas to make Mexico City. Once your story is known, Cordovan will be just another exiled general."

Smiley Lassiter slid from the pilot's seat, and Baldez took his place.

Carter took Lupe Vargas's elbow and guided her a few feet from the others. He pressed an envelope in her hand and smiled.

"It's all there. I'll see you in Zurich in a month."

She nodded, brushed his lips with hers, and ran back to the chopper.

They watched it lift off and head west, toward Mexico City. When it was out of sight, Carter turned to the others.

"You all know where to pick up your money."

The five men shook each other's hands and disappeared into the night.

EIGHTEEN

Benito Venezzio cursed and threw the newspaper across the room.

The news was bitter. General Cordovan had been shot by his own officers when news had reached the capital that Ramón Baldez was alive and safe. Baldez had returned to Guatemala and formed a new government.

That had been nearly a month ago, and still no word.

"The bitch," he hissed, "she has double crossed me! She's somewhere in the world right now with the money, laughing at me. The bitch, the whore, I was a fool to trust her!"

Venezzio stood and walked toward the terrace. He paused as he passed a mirror and examined his face.

The bandages were off. He had healed quickly. He could barely discern the scars.

He had a new face, a new name, and no money.

"The bitch . . . the whore!"

A sound from below brought him out onto the terrace. He pulled the Beretta from his belt and held it at his side. An old man was walking around the empty swimming pool.

"Who are you?"

"You called my company for an estimate on repairing the pool, senhor."

"Oh, yes, I thought I canceled that."

The old man shrugged. "I wasn't told. I have the figure. You are Senhor Luigi Antonelli?" He waved a piece of paper up at the terrace. Venezzio looked from him over the hillside of vines and on to the winery.

A new life with no running, he thought. *I don't have enough money to put water in the pool even if it were repaired.*

The whore . . . the bitch!

Suddenly he laughed. "Yes, I am Senhor Luigi Antonelli. Bring the damned paper up here."

"*Sim, senhor.*"

Venezzio moved back into the room and poured brandy into a glass. When the knock came at the door, he carried the glass with him.

He left the Beretta on the bar.

"Yes, give . . ."

The old man was no longer stooped nor was he old. He stood upright, a pistol held in both hands.

"*Ciao*, Benito."

There were two shots, but Venezzio heard neither of them.

One never hears the sound of the shot that kills one.

Carter dropped the Stechkin on the floor and left the villa.

NINETEEN

Herr Bernard Mueller, executive director of the Banque Suiss Nationale, pulled the last paper back across the desk and beamed at the beautiful raven-haired woman sitting across from him.

"Will that be all?" she asked.

"*Ja*, Fraülein Navarro, everything is in order. And I want to thank you very much. The funds will be transferred into your country's European account within the hour."

"And you will send confirmation to President Baldez?"

"Certainly."

She stood, and it was all Mueller could do to keep his eyes off her stunning figure.

"It has been a pleasure, Herr Mueller."

"It has indeed," he beamed. "Good day."

"Good day."

She left the office, and from the bank walked into the bright noontime sun above Zurich.

He was waiting on the corner.

"Good day, Señorita Dominique Navarro."

"Good day, Mr. Jules Blackmer. You look well."

"Portugal was good for the soul."

They linked arms and began to stroll down the wide boulevard.

193

"I trust *your* business went well?" he said.

"Oh, yes. The treasury of my country is healthy again."

"Excellent. Now, tell me, what would you like to see most, the scintillating sights of Zurich . . . or the ceiling of my suite?"

She laughed and hugged him. "Do you have to ask?"

DON'T MISS THE NEXT NEW NICK CARTER SPY THRILLER

THE TERROR CODE

They parked a block from the building, and by instinct, Carter checked their perimeter as they covered the distance and moved into the narrow lobby.

"Something?" Jennifer asked.

Carter shrugged. "Habit. Remember, somebody went through his hotel room."

An elevator made a slow, laborious climb to the fifth floor; they could have walked faster. Jennifer stepped out first and nodded toward a door at the end of an empty hall.

Carter could barely make out a small American flag on the bottom right-hand corner of the door's pane. Across its center, in small letters in both Arabic and English, he read: Military Disbursements U.S. Navy.

"We're a little late," Jennifer said, reaching for the knob. "She's probably already here." The door opened easily to her touch. She preceded Carter by a step, and came up short. "Oh, my God."

Carter muscled by her, tugging his favorite lady, Wilhelmina—a 9mm Luger—from the shoulder rig under his left armpit.

One look said it all.

There was a jumble of papers and file cards strewn across the floor of the outer office. There was a single desk, a pair of tumbled chairs, and tipped file cabinets.

In the middle of it all lay a young woman wearing jeans and a sweatshirt with Georgetown printed across its front.

Carter took one side, Jennifer the other. Blood spilled down the left side of the young woman's face from a nasty cut above her eye. She was awake and groaning, trying to rise. Carter had no doubt that this was the lieutenant they were supposed to meet.

Carter cradled her with his free arm. "What happened, Lieutenant?"

"Came in, somebody hit me . . ."

The Killmaster turned her slightly. He waved the Luger toward two closed doors at right angles to each other across the room. "What's in there?"

"Lieutenant Commander Harris's office . . . spare office," she replied, her voice barely a whisper.

"Are they connected?" Carter asked.

As the dazed woman nodded dumbly, there was the sound of a drawer hitting the floor in one of the offices. It brought Carter to his feet.

"Take care of her, and stay down!" he hissed at Jennifer.

He moved across the room at a crouch and tested the door. The knob turned, but there was something holding it closed from the other side.

He couldn't budge it, but the sound of the knob turning brought a bullet tearing through the door at about where Carter's gut would have been if he hadn't been practically on his knees.

Keeps, Carter thought. *Whoever they are, they're playing for keeps. And whatever they're after, they want it bad.*

He rolled to the second door and went through on his belly. The connecting door between the two offices was open a crack. He saw a man going through the rear window onto a fire escape balcony.

Carter started to lurch forward, when three more slugs raised hell with the plaster not a foot from his side.

The Killmaster got off one shot as the figure disappeared from sight, going down.

He rushed to the open window and peered cautiously over the sill.

The guy was tall and lean with dark hair, long, runner's legs visible beneath a flowing djellaba. Carter couldn't see his face.

He had dropped to a balcony a floor below, then jumped to an adjoining rooftop. Right now he was racing for another roof as Carter squeezed off two more from the Luger.

One of the slugs hit the tar, but Carter was sure he winged the man with the other. The runner grabbed his arm, twisted, and fell.

But as the Killmaster jumped the railing, the fleeing man stumbled back to his feet and continued across the roof and over the edge without firing another shot.

Carter estimated he could easily outrun the man once he got over the roof himself. But his quarry seemed to know the layout of the buildings and moved down the fragile balconies with surprising ease considering he had a bullet hole in the right shoulder and was wearing a flowing, loose-fitting djellaba, though the garment didn't seem to slow him down much.

How in the name of God did he manage to move so easily in that thing? Carter wondered as he made his way down the side of the second building in time to see the trespasser heading for a crowd swarming through an entrance to the Medina. He could have been swallowed up in the sea of people in the same loose-fitting garments of varying shades of gray and brown . . . except that Carter spotted an ever-widening crimson stain on the man's right shoulder.

Carter's six-foot-plus height allowed him to see easily over the heads of the crowd as he raced down the stone steps. Keeping his quarry in sight, he stumbled over and nearly fell into an assortment of candies and nuts spread out around a vendor sitting cross-legged in the dirt at a busy intersection. He regained his balance in time to see the red-stained djellaba make an abrupt turn to the right, so he edged forward as fast as possible against the press of the crowd.

At the corner, Carter turned right, relieved to see his man still stumbling along ahead. He was slowed often along the shadowed street by people seated at shin level and oranges displayed at hip level. The gap was widening and Carter didn't like it. He saw what looked like an opening in a group of ambling peddlers, did a swivel-hipped couple of steps, and still tumbled over a group of veiled woman huddled on the narrow walk against a stone wall.

Instantly he was surrounded by scowling men.

"*Pardon, pardon,*" Carter growled, getting to his feet and through them before someone could start some serious retaliation.

Up ahead, on a street that slanted deeper and deeper into the bowels of the old city, the man turned left.

He's moving more slowly because of that arm, Carter thought jubilantly. But then he, too, seemed to be making less headway. When he got to the turnoff street, it was vacant except for a few children bouncing a ball against the whitewashed walls. The emptiness was a stark contrast to the throng on the main drag.

Carter took advantage of it and raced down the narrow confines, around a curve that brought him to an abrupt halt.

The street he was on went straight ahead into a deserted residential path, high walls shielding the innards of houses from view. A crossway veered off to the left and right. For as far as he could see in either direction, women in tentlike white garments and men in djellabas moved casually at a pace much slower than that in the main streets. There was no sight of anyone rushing or trying to avoid notice, or of anyone in a blood-stained garment or attempting to hide one.

Carter hesitated only a few seconds before moving decisively to the left. When he found nothing, he retraced his steps and went off to the right. Again he retraced, and hurried straight ahead.

Cursing himself for his inability to do what he deemed a simple job, he was ready to give up and head back, when a small splotch of blood on the ground caught his eye. Pulse quickening, he moved slowly, spotting another and another and another. That shoulder wound must have brushed against something to cause the sudden bleeding. Or maybe the man, unable to hold his hand against his chest any longer, had allowed it to drop to his side and a build-up of blood was trickling down his arm.

The trail led to another intersection, which Carter approached cautiously. But there seemed no danger as he

peered around the corner, so he moved on. He passed a
group of men talking and suddenly realized that the
blood spots had disappeared.

He backtracked, but there was no doorway in the im-
mediate vicinity. He stood puzzled as the group broke
up, the men going off in different directions. It was then
he caught sight of the freshly beheaded chicken one man
carried by the feet . . . the crimson droplets falling at his
side.

"Shit," Carter hissed aloud, and looked around for a
tall landmark that would lead him back to the Rue
Mauriac.

—from THE TERROR CODE
A New Nick Carter Spy Thriller
From Charter in April 1987